A LAUGH OUT LOUD HOLIDAY ROMANCE

my billionaire fake fiance

BY

LINDA WEST

Manufactured in the United Stated of America

10 9 8 7 6 5 4 3 2 1

First Edition

Copyright@LindaWest

For my dear sister Cheryl

PUBLISHING BOOKS GOOD FOR THE SOUL

Other books by Linda West

Death by Rolling Pin

Death by Crockpot

The Magical Christmas Do-Over

Christmas Kisses and Cookies

Holiday Wishes and Valentine Kisses

Olympic Wishes and Easter Kisses

Firework Wishes and Summertime Kisses

Paris Wishes and Christmas Kisses

Christmas Belles and Mistletoe Kisses

Hello!

It's the Christmas season, the happiest time of the year! Before we begin, let's get you settled in with a cup of cocoa and a comfy chair. Let's imagine a crackling fire is beside you casting a warmth and glow. Perhaps a light snow has begun to fall outside. When Christmas is upon us and joy fills the air, we remember that all good things are possible. So, sit back, relax, and have a nice drink. You're about to take a wonderful fun-filled adventure with the adorable inhabitants of the Christmas-obsessed town of Kissing Bridge. Now on to the story, I hope you enjoy it.

Sending you love and cheer and mistletoe wishes. May your days be filled with Christmas cookies and kisses!

With love,
Linda West

Don't forget to look in the back to get my
best-selling book
Christmas Kisses and Cookies

FOR FREE!

Happy holidays!

Chapter 1

"**W**HAT IS THIS?" I screamed to no one, because I was

the only person crazy enough to be outside in this
snowstorm.
The driving snow gusts whipped me in the face, and I
regretted that I was too vain to wear one of those face
sweaters that make you look like a hoodlum.
    I slid my backpack off and threw it on top of the snow,
ready to do battle. I wiggled the post of the *For Sale* sign
on our lawn back and forth and attempted to unleash it
from the ice that had formed around the base. I couldn't

believe someone would play a joke like this—especially around Christmas.

I scanned the neighborhood for possible offenders before spotting Mr. Aikens through the sheets of white, shoveling his car out of his driveway next door. He looked innocent enough. Even if he didn't donate to my *Save the Trees Campaign.*

I waved. He waved back and shouted, "Hey, Allie. I spotted you down the block. Was that an Uber car you got out of?"

I gritted my teeth and looked back over my shoulder at my drop off point. I concocted a little fib because I couldn't tell Mr. Aikens the truth, or he'd blab it to my father for sure. They played bocce ball every Wednesday. I swear those older men gossip more than my girlfriends.

"No, of course not. Ex-Boyfriend—boyfriend's car…"

I still hadn't gotten used to the *ex* part, although I should have it tattooed on my forehead by now.

"Go out with me, and I promise you'll leave me for someone better."

My ex, Shane, had *officially* left me two years ago, one day after my mother lost her long battle with cancer. I still hadn't the heart to tell my dad that Shane had left me when I needed him most. I kept saying he was busy. It was hard enough for me to deal with the fact he had bailed on me at the worst time of my life. At twenty-seven, I wasn't old enough to be jaded, but honestly, I was scarred.

I continued my struggle with the unwanted sign and wondered again who had the nerve to put up a *For Sale* sign in our yard? I had heard prices had been going up on the Jersey Shore, so maybe some overly zealous realtor made a mistake?

I called out through the whistling snow flurries. "Mr. Aikens, by any chance do you know who put this sign up?"

Mr. Aikens looked over with a tilt of his head to study the oddity. "Nope."

Humph. Now I was officially annoyed. I finally got on both sides of the darn sign and tugged straight up with all my force. It gave loose suddenly, of course, with my last thrust and sent me flying across the yard a good three feet. I landed with a thud on my back and the stupid sign on top of me. I wrestled it off and dusted off the snow.

"Need help?' Mr. Aikens offered now.

"No, no, I got it, thanks."

I stood up and gathered my sense of humor, and my backpack. If I had seen anyone else do this, I would have laughed my butt off. Since it was me, I wasn't as amused.

"Well, Merry Christmas to you, Allie." Mr. Aikens smiled. "You tell your father hello for me."

"I will. Merry Christmas to you and Mrs. Aikens."

I waved goodbye as I started the trudge up our tundra-like driveway with the hated sign tucked under my arm.

When I found out who did this, they were going to hear it from me.

I tossed the offensive sign in the garage and shut the door. It was time to lie to my father. He'd ask me where Shane was, and I'd say I took the bus because Shane was busy– *again*.

The honest to goodness truth is, *I did take Uber*. I'm broke as heck, but I couldn't deal with the train-bus-train combo I'd have to endure. Christmas was always tough emotionally since mom passed, and I didn't need to freak out over a little Uber.

It's all Shane's fault, anyway, as far as I'm concerned. He's the one who talked me into college in the city–how romantic—driving together and forever after. All of those were lies! He left me for an Icelandic blonde intern at the dean's office! He said she was polished and perfect and he had fallen in love by mistake.

By mistake?

To add insult to injury, he had also stopped driving me to college at the request of Ms. Sweden. This is why I had to deal with the dreaded bus-train combo and ultimately be lying to my father and my neighbor right now.

This is why I hate men.

You give them everything, and then they disappear like a leech full of blood that falls off when it's done using you.

That is why if this were a real love story, my true love would be Uber. Uber has never let me down. Uber is always there for me. Uber does not prefer Icelandic blondes. I'm no Einstein, but I know that *falling in love with an inanimate object is far safer than falling in love with a man.*

Chapter 2

*U*nfortunately, my affair with Uber is an unrequited love since my family is in the car service business. Sadly, the company profits from Archer Premier Transport had been cut in half due to the arrival of my perfect Uberian love. The mega driving service had, without a doubt, revolutionized travel in the modern world.

I opened the side door, and Christmas music welcomed me in. The archway had been newly lit with twinkly lights and mistletoe. My stomach did that pit-drop thing it does whenever I feel something. I realized it was the decorations.

We had always done them together, but now Dad must have put them up for me. I took a deep breath. Christmas had a way of bringing up all the memories people tried to shut away.

Dad was in the middle of stirring something in a big pot when I came into the kitchen. I guessed it was Hungarian goulash, which was his signature and only complicated dish.

He had a defeated slump to his stirring. I kissed him on the cheek and threw my purse on the chair, which elicited a big, resentful *meow!*

My cat, Piewacket, leapt off the chair and gave me the evil cat-eye. It's not my fault her brown-toned fur blends in with all the colonial furniture! I've sat on her numerous times. I should get her a white collar.

"Sorry, Pie," I called over. She resent-meowed back at me and sashayed out of the room.

I pulled off my snowcap and ran my hands through my tangle of mousy hair. It was flat at the top where my cap has crushed it, and no amount of fluffing was rectifying that today.

"Dad, did you know someone put up a *For Sale* sign on the lawn?"

He stopped stirring and stared out the window at the falling snow.

"Dad–did you hear me?" I asked. He finally looked at me and shook his head. Uh oh. His eyes were *navy tone.*

Dad is the easiest person to read. He has amazing blue eyes, which change like a mood ring. His eyes can go from joyous royal blue to peaceful cerulean blue, to serious deep blue to this–*crisis* navy blue color they were now.

"Dad, what's wrong?"

"I didn't want to worry you, Allie." I felt this ominous cloud hit me. He put down the ladle and hung his head.

"After your mom got sick, I leveraged everything we had to help with the hospital bills, but it wasn't enough on any account…" He paused. "We're…I'm losing the house."

I froze.

"Wait –are you saying *you* put the *For Sale* sign up?"

He nodded sadly.

I threw my hands up. "You have got to be kidding me! I can't believe you'd even think about this!"

"I have no choice. I'm sorry, Allie. We have to sell or they'll foreclose on it. If I sell now while the area is hot, maybe I can save some of my investment and the business."

"You leveraged Archer Premier as well?"

He nodded.

I tried to make sense of this, but it was shocking. Dad had never mentioned money problems before. Sure, I knew things had been tight because of the medical bills, but I had no idea it had gotten so bad.

"Dad, we can't sell Mom's house!

A tear sprang to his eyes. "I've been trying to save it, honey. I just haven't been able to catch up. This is my last resort."

I looked around the living room I knew like the back of my hand. The sunflower stencils Mom and I had done…the penciled graph on the wall of me growing, or not–I had hoped for more than my five-foot-three but, alas, it was not to be. The fake Christmas tree we'd had as long as I could remember…I loved this house. I had planned to live here for the rest of my life.

I began to hyperventilate, which is my go-to panic attack coping mechanism.

Dad came over and wrapped his beefy arms around me.

"Breathe, Allie. Breathe."

I sucked in deep breaths, and I sniffed in his Old Spice cologne that Mom had gotten for him every year at Christmas. I wondered if he was running out. Two years now. Mental note—*get more Old Spice*. Never thought I'd say that.

"Mr. Somerset mentioned the Carriage House being available. He's very generous. Of course, it's much farther from the college…"

"There is no way we are taking charity from the Somersets, Dad. I hate them." I pulled back and Betty-Booped him with my own big, blue-eyed look that meant I was serious.

"Dad, I thought the business was doing fine. You never mentioned…"

"People don't need private cars anymore; they take Uber. Thankfully we have the Somersets, or we would go under just like all the other car services."

I swallowed my guilt and promised myself I would delete my Uber app as soon as I was alone.

"What can we do now? I want to help."

He looked me in the face, and a half-smile lifted the side of his full lips that didn't quite make it to his eyes. "We can move on, darling. A house is not home–*a home is where the heart is…*"

I repeated the words with him.

My mother had always said that. But the only thing we had left to show she had lived, loved, and made a place for her heart was right here. *I'd be darned if I ever let this house go.*

I wiped away a tear with an irritating swipe of the hand. "I'll put off finishing college. I can get a full-time job or work with you–whatever it takes. How much do we need to save the house?"

He let out a deep huff of defeat. "Two hundred thousand dollars."

"Two hundred thousand dollars?" I reeled.

He nodded.

"Did you just say two hundred thousand dollars?" Full Betty-Boop eyes now.

"Yep, that's right. Two hundred thousand dollars."

"Two hundred thousand dollars!" My heart sank. The staggering sum deflated my optimism like a prick to a balloon. Impossible.

I squeezed my eyes tight. I worked part time as a waitress at the Caddy Shack, but it barely paid for my books and mounting college bills. How the heck was I going to help find two hundred thousand dollars?

Two hundred thousand dollars.
Two hundred thousand dollars.
Two hundred thousand dollars.

I wracked my brains. How does one get money like that when they need it?

Chapter 3

"*I* assume you tried to leverage the house—" I began.

Dad went back to stirring the goulash. "I've taken out three loans on the house, honey. We're loaned out."

"Anything we can take out of Archer Transport?"

He glanced at me with his guilt royal blue orbs. "As much as I could without losing it."

I let out my breath. I was not overly smart, and this was beyond my thinking capacity. I was running out of options.

"Do we have any rich friends I don't know about?" I asked with hope.

Dad shook his head. "Not that I know of."

"What about in the movies when those gamblers get into trouble? They always find some seedy guy to loan them money. I wonder how they go about getting two hundred thousand dollars?"

Dad shrugged. "Not sure how to go about soliciting the mob."

I made a mental note to ask the cook at work, Frankie Musso, if he had any connects. He always bragged about being from Sicily. I wondered if inquiring about mob connections would be considered offensive. Not that I care about civilities now.

Still, it was a loan. I would have to pay the mob back sometime. I wondered what the penalty would be if you didn't pay back the mob. Would they kill me, or maybe just break my leg so I could pay them later? Two hundred thousand dollars for a broken leg seemed fair.

I imagined myself with a broken leg taking one for the team. It wouldn't be pleasant, but I wasn't an athlete or anything, so I could deal with a hobble for six months until it healed.

I did wonder how exactly they would go about the process of breaking my leg, though. Would they shoot it with a gun, or just hit my poor kneecap with a big bat? The mob guys on TV seemed to use bats a lot. Then again, who's to say they'd stop at one leg?

Maybe two hundred thousand dollars with no payback would mean a double leg breaking. I looked down at my innocent legs and rubbed them. I suddenly had more appreciation for my limbs.

I needed some creative way to get the two hundred grand—*without* needing to pay it back.

A college pal, Tammy Hines, put her virginity up for sale to the highest bidder on Facebook to pay for her tuition.

I wondered what that total had come to and if Tammie had shared it in her Saturday morning confessional at St. Paul's. Not sure how many rosaries that would come to. Maybe that's why I hadn't seen her lately.

I'd have to call her later in any case because desperate times called for desperate measures– and I liked my legs.

A happy Christmas song came on in the background and I choked up. This was so messed up. Christmas had always been my favorite time of year. We made cookies and homemade gifts for each other like we were in some Rockwell sketch. Now everything had a gray veil over it, like the whole photo album of memories had been switched to monotones.

Dad spooned goulash into Christmas bowls decorated with bells and elves. He put them on the table and plopped down beside me. The spicy stew wafted up and my stomach grumbled. I blew on my goulash and took a big spoonful.

"Good?" he queried.

I smiled. "Awesome as usual."

Dad grew the tomatoes himself in the back office, along with multiple herbs during the winter months. It was his passion. I could taste a hint of the basil and its fresh bite against the heavier flavors.

"Good job with the lemon basil–nice touch."

He glowed and took another spoonful.

I glanced around the kitchen and the twinkly lights that rimmed the ceiling—we pulled them out every year during the holidays. We lived a middle-income, cozy life, and I had always been fine with that. Now for the first time I wanted more. I wanted that two hundred grand.

"Dad, I just don't get the world! We're good people with good morals, how come we aren't getting rewarded for it?'

"We have each other …"

"I know, and I'm grateful, but I'm talking about money! How come all of the mean people have all the money?"

He let out his breath as he added some pepper to his goulash. "You can't change the world, Allie."

I cocked my head to the side. I'd given up on men, but I wasn't about to give up on the world. I still had hope that if I threw all my energy into helping the world, I'd live a life well lived. Maybe get a park dedicated to me with my name on it. Better yet, buy the rainforest in the Amazon and protect it forever. I took in a deep breath. It did sound impossible.

"Maybe I'll double down on the scratch offs and get lucky. I brought you some home by the way—they're in my backpack."

Dad's eyebrows rose and he got up from the table. He just loved his scratch offs.

"They're in the side pocket," I called over.
He fished them out and held them up triumphantly.

"Thanks, honey. Maybe we'll get lucky."

He brought them back to the table and pulled out his lucky quarter and got scratching.

"I don't know, maybe I should think outside the box – what would I do if I wasn't a nice Catholic girl?"

Dad looked up from rubbing off the scratch ticket. "You mean like be a stripper?"

"What? No! I'm saying we're not going to lose this place. Okay? I don't know how, but I'll figure it out."

Dad scratched off the last lotto tickets and shook his head. "Better luck next time."

I pondered my spoonful of goulash and wondered when our *next time* would come.

Chapter 4

"*I* saw on TV that a bunch of people got arrested in a protest in front of the Somerset building–please tell me you weren't there." My dad had his serious eyeshade going–azure.

My face flamed and I made a production of loving my goulash. "Yum!" I said instead of fibbing anymore.

Of course I was there. I organized the darn fair wage protest! Somerset Industries made a fortune and paid their workers less than other prominent companies in the area.

The truth was I had bumped straight into the heir to the Somerset Throne before the police pulled me away–with a warning.

I glanced at the clock. "You better get ready to go to the center, Dad—I put your Santa outfit on the hanger in the guest room. That tummy takes up a lot of room." I laughed.

Argument deflected.

Dad's phone chirped and he put a finger up and lowered his voice to his professional tone. I recognized the ring. Mr. Moneybags on the redline.

"Hello, Mr. Somerset. Of course. Right away."

Chapter 5

1 cleaned up our dishes and helped myself to some

chocolate milk. The snowstorm outside looked like it had gone code red. I could barely see our birdbath in the backyard.

I cast a glance at Dad's serious expression as he paced and listened. Stupid Somersets. I hated them. They were everything I abhorred about humanity. They were also my family's benefactors in a way. Sigh.

The blue-blood Somerset's were THE SOMERSETS of Long Island's old money, and also owners of Somerset Enterprises. They had made their billions in multiple areas, but the most significant was in boxes.

They were the providers for Bamazon, and the online retail business kept going straight up along with their need for boxes.

The youngest Somerset, Devlin, had taken over the reins a bit ago and had been credited for steering the bulk of their assets into the box realm. As the world became more delivery orientated, the need for boxes had grown and grown, and with it, their fortune. They owned half of the trees in America and employed people all over the country.

The royal Somersets were also and had always been Dad's biggest client. He had chauffeured Mr. and Mrs. Somerset and their children since they were born. We had lived on the extensive property when I was a child back in the days when carriage houses still had a place in proper society. And until the spoiled Sissy Somerset decided that our home should be *her* art studio and we had to move.

In the end, the change had been the best thing for us. Dad bought us our own home here on the Jersey Shore, and we had started a new venture. As well as being the premier chauffeur for the Somersets and keeping their cars in order, Dad and Mom had invested in more cars over the years and started Archer Premier Transport.

Dad came back into the kitchen, looking troubled. I was afraid to ask.

He finally blew out his breath and released a short laugh. "Well, when it rains, it pours, doesn't it, darling? Or when it snows, it blizzards, in this case." He cut a glance at the snow-packed window.

I looked up from petting Piewacket, who was sprawled on my lap. "What did the Superior Somersets need from you *today?*" I said in my fake haughty voice.

"Mr. Somerset has decided he would like to go out–despite the conditions. I'm going to have to call the center and tell them I won't be there to play Santa tonight this year."

I sprang to my feet in battle mode, and Piewacket fell off my lap. She was beyond irritated with me again, but I didn't have time for her. There was no way the Somersets were ruining my mom's special holiday function she had started! It was a tradition!

Ooooh, it was sooooo typical of the Somersets to call last minute and ruin everything!

"Dad, no–just say no."

"It's okay, darling. I don't feel much up to ho-ho-hoing, anyway." The sadness in his eyes showed that wasn't the truth.

I put my hands on my hips. "No, no, no, no! The homeless center holiday party was so important to Mom. I know it's always been important to you too!"

I pointed out the window at the dire weather. "They've been issuing no driving warnings all over the news—they can call somebody else! Just say no, Dad."

Dad patted me on the back. "Yes, they can call somebody else, honey, but if they start calling another car service, or worse, Uber, I will lose my biggest client. I can't say no to the Somersets."

Another Christmas interrupted by those overindulged Somersets. How many holidays or special occasions were interrupted because the Somersets called?

"Dad, they don't care about other people. They don't care that maybe you were spending Christmas morning with your child or your sick wife, they just—"

"Allie, stop, darling. I appreciate the Somersets. They gave us a great life, and it's not their fault we lost your mother."

It was just too much. Mom gone, our home about to be lost—and the homeless center holiday party without their Santa? Maybe I couldn't change everything, but I could save Mom's legacy and a little child's dream at Christmas.

"Who called? Which one is it—the old man?"

Dad smiled. "No, he's been out of town for a long while now. It's Devlin."

Oh, of course. Devlin. Figures. Who goes out in the middle of a snowstorm anyway? Devlin Somerset, because the weather stops in his wake.

"Seriously, where does he need to go in this crazy blizzard?"

"Not for me to ask, darling. My job is to drive."

"Dad, just let me go drive him. I'll go take the spoiled brat where he needs to get dropped off. He's probably going to the 21 clubs, or a strip club, more likely, knowing Devlin."

I pushed on when my Dad hesitated. "You just said yourself we can't afford to lose the Somersets as clients. I'm home now, and I'm going to help, and I'm going to start by doing what Mom would've liked. You're going give out the toys tonight, and I'm going drive the self-centered brat."

Dad scratched his head and I rushed on.

"I've been driving for you practically since I could drive. I can certainly take Mr. Fancy-Pants around town or whatever he needs. He never even looks through the darn divider window; he probably won't even know it's not you!"

Dad laughed at that thought. Despite the fact I refused to wear makeup or mess with my locks, my father still considered me a natural beauty. I'm not. I like my smile but the rest of me is just average.

In any case, Devlin Somerset might be blind enough to his own narcissism that he wouldn't even notice. Dad seemed to consider it.

I pushed him toward the back room and the awaiting Santa Suit.

"Look—go to the center, and I'll meet you there. I'm sure I'll be back in a snap, and we'll celebrate together."

He seemed doubtful, but I was not about to leave the kids disappointed.

"Please, don't leave the kids hanging. You know how much they count on this—we might not be able to do anything about some things, but we can make a difference tonight. You know Mom would want you to be there."

Dad eyes softened –light blue. He knew I was right. Devlin rarely left the Upper East Side, so it was sure to be a quick ride.

"I wish I had somebody else—but with this blizzard coming and all the airports closed…" He looked doubtful, but I could see he was relenting.

"Of course, I always have their Rolls Royce Limo ready, so that's thankfully not an issue."
Dad's face clouded with doubt. "Are you sure…?"

I held out my hand. "Give me the address."
I wasn't taking no for an answer.

He inhaled deeply and reached in his pocket, producing the pickup location. He handed it over tentatively.

"Okay, darling. I have a uniform that should fit you. It won't be perfect." His brow furrowed.

"Don't worry, Dad. He won't even know it's me, and I'll be back before you can say jingle bells."

Chapter 6

1 pulled the chauffeur cap over my piled-up hair and

tucked in a stray lock. No matter how much I adjusted the overly big uniform, I still looked like Tom Hanks in *Big*.

The bellboy of the Chic Park Avenue Elite Apartments opened the side limo door as Devlin Somerset strode out of the glass entrance with a statuesque blonde bombshell gliding behind him.

I kept my head down as I glanced at the handsome man in the Gucci suit and elegant tweed coat draped over his shoulder as if he were an off-duty superhero.

Devlin Somerset was a chiseled work of man-art that was for sure. Even as a child, he had been overly cute. Now that he was grown, he was tall with imposing shoulders that made everything he wore an instant fashion statement.

I studied him in the side mirror as they approached. Everything about him screamed *rich.* He was tanned despite the weather, and his gray eyes were enough to make any girl go soft inside. He had graced the cover of GQ and been named the *World's Sexiest Man*, but I knew firsthand what a spoiled jerk he really was.

I cast my eyes down and pulled in my breath as Devlin and his date slipped into the back seat. If I were lucky, they'd never even notice I wasn't my father driving as usual.

I glanced briefly into the rearview mirror to see if I had been detected, but thankfully Devlin was caught up in his voluptuous platinum-haired bombshell in the back seat. She was kissing him as his hand ran up her leg like ice cream.

The bellboy opened the door and handed me an address. "Mr. Somerset will be vacationing at his family Ski Chalet in the mountains for a holiday. This is the address."

I nodded like I imagined my father would and looked at the paper with the address. My eyes widened.

Kissing Bridge—Vermont!

Vermont?!

Seriously?

My heart quickened. Vermont was five hours away! I took a deep breath, but my heart sank. I would never

make it back in time for the holiday party tonight! I
wanted to groan, but I was afraid Devlin might hear.

I considered my options while Devlin's face was busy
buried in his date's massive bosoms. I really wanted to
know how long he planned to STAY in Vermont. Gosh,
darn it. Drivers drove. They didn't question their bosses'
choices. I had promised Dad I would handle it.

I glanced out at the inclement weather, unsure of
traversing dangerous mountain roads in a Rolls Royce limo
with no tire bands. New York City streets were one thing,
but the ski mountains of Vermont were an entirely
different story.

There was a heavy rap on the dividing window and I
jumped like a ninny.

"Let's get a move on, Charles, I'd rather not be caught in
the blizzard on this side of the mountainside," Devlin said.

I groaned and put the Rolls into gear.

Chapter 7

"*W*hat do you want me to act like, Grandma Moses?"

Miss ample bosoms squealed in the back.

I watched the road, but I peeled my ears.

The sound was on in the back so I could be of service if they needed me, but it also allowed me to hear everything they were saying. I considered turning off the sound but decided against it. Maybe I could sell a story to the tabloids for some cash? At the very least it would be entertaining.

Devlin was being charming and trying to calm his Latina Goddess's temper down. "No, just clothes that cover your body. I don't want you to get frostbite, darling..."

She was angry with him, and I was loving listening to Mr. Man *squirm*.

"Oh, you thought it was fine when you met me when I had no clothes on my body."

Devlin cleared his throat uncomfortably. "Look, my father is very traditional. I told you to wear the clothes that I bought you. Did you even pack them?"

"I gave them to my maid. They old people's clothes. I no wear that! Why should I cover up my body? My body is my *gift*. Do you not *love* my gift? Others *love* my gift!"

I rolled my eyes and faked a cough to cover the little laugh that came out. I couldn't help, but sneak peeks at the drama ensuing in the back. Served him right that Devlin. Spoiled brat. He'd been getting anything he wanted since he took his first golden breath.

Sofia had large full lips that were now pouted in displeasure and steam rose up her cheeks. Devlin was petting her like a miniature Chihuahua.

"Listen, Sofia, we went over this and over this." Devlin cooed. "Please, just please get through this next four days with me, and I'll give you whatever you want."

My mouth dropped at the mention of four days.

FOUR DAYS?!

Sofia seemed mollified by a bribe.
"Whatever I *want*?" She tinkled out.
"Yes - whatever you want."
"I want a *lot*."
"You always *do*."

"Maybe this time we can get me a pair of boobs that include cleavage. Is that too much to ask? Stupid New York surgeons…I should move back to Spain…"

He poured her a drink and rubbed her shoulders. "Just take a little stress off, but remember don't drink too much and don't talk about all the free sexual encounters you've had."

Sofia blew up. "My work is art! Do you want me to be somebody else? You don't love me!" She squealed out. Devlin went back to petting her again.

"Of course, I just… I'm just saying my father is difficult – We just need to get in and get out. If he thinks I am finally marrying and settling down, he's more likely to give me what I want."

I sucked in my breath. Wow this was really getting good. I bet the *Tattler* would give me a whole heap of cash to hear about this intimate exchange. If I could only have secretly videoed this, it would be worth a fortune. I considered taking notes, but I was driving, so I just peeled my ears for details.

"So, I'm supposed to act? I'm just an *act* for you? I'm just a *play* thing?" Sofia rage was on the rise and building up steam.

"No – well you're an actress, right?" Devlin countered. "Nothing wrong with acting."
I'm just asking you to be yourself, but *acting* self."

Oh, this was rich. I had to give it to Devlin. He was smooth. Still, Sofia looked like Mt. Vesuvius ready to explode, and I couldn't wait for the finale of these fireworks.

"I'm just asking you to subdue some of your more passionate side. I need him to trust me -this is good for both of us, baby."

"Good for *you*. Not good for *me*!"

Devlin let out a loud gush of air and held up her hand. "You have the biggest diamond ever! Why can't you just be happy and do what I want?"

"Happy? You think I wanted a *thing*? You *never* give me what I want! I want a commitment. Why not this Christmas, we set a real date for our wedding to make your father so happy for real?"

Devlin threw his hands up in the air. "I'm just not ready to set a date. We've talked about this."

"ARGGGGG!" The scream of agitation from the beauty was piercing. I turned the sound down and shook out my eardrums, but I didn't turn the sound off.

"Sofia, come on honey. I'll buy you that diamond necklace you wanted at Tiffany's?"

Sofia considered it. "And the matching earrings?"

Devlin blew hard out his nose. "Some women don't need to be paid to accompany their boyfriend to meet his parents!"

"Ahh, but you want me to be an actress – act like someone else – like someone you marry. But me not good enough to marry?"

Devlin shrugged. "I didn't think you believed in marriage, Sofia, that's why I asked you to marry me! "

My mouth fell open and made a little "o."
There it was. Typical guy. They were all the same. But Sofia wasn't having any of it.
"You want to buy me and use me up and then I be old and never be marriage material?"

Devlin cocked his head to one side. "Let's face it, Sofia. A porn star isn't the career you go into if you want a traditional life. That's why we're so good baby – come on I'll get you the earrings too. I promise." But Sofia had worked herself into a full Latino hand-throwing tirade.

Devlin caught my eye in the mirror and angrily reached over and shut off the sound button. I blushed and focused on the road. Gosh darn it, right when it was getting good.

I refocused on the road instead of the drama, ensuring in the back of the limo. But, suddenly there was an angry pounding on the divider window.

"Stop, stop, stop, stop!" Sofia rapped on the divider window rapidly to get my attention.
I slowed down and turned slightly, trying to keep my face undercover and be of service to the woman who was now screaming in complete Spanish—which I couldn't understand through the divider window or otherwise, as I didn't speak any other languages.

I looked at the switch to pull it down and gritted my teeth. If I turned around, they'd know for sure that I wasn't my dad.

I had hoped to be far out of Manhattan before they realized their usual driver had been replaced and by then it would be too late to do anything about it. I was unsure of what to do.

"Little, short un-attractive woman driver. Stop Now! I demand of you! "She screamed.
I reluctantly turned to see her face pushed up against the window. Close up, her big fake lips resembled a potato man add-on feature.

I grudgingly rolled down the window between us as slowly as possible, but I kept driving. I hoped Devlin would offer her a better deal or more jewelry or something that would pacify her and we could just get on with this.

Devlin was all butter. But, Sofia was done.
"Just settle down, honey. We'll work this out. Keep driving."

That's when Sofia took it to another level. She rolled down her back window and stuck her head out.

"Rape! Rape! Help me! Help me! I demand you pull over now!"

I rolled my eyes and pulled over to the side of the road. Before the limo was fully stopped, Sofia flung open her door with a bang.

"You want an actress, you can find another one. You have no heart, Devlin Somerset. We done."

With that, she tugged the colossal engagement ring off her hand and threw it hard at Devlin's head. It bounced off his cleft chin, leaving a little red blood spot. He raised a hand to his perfectly chiseled face, bewildered.

Sofia stepped off the curb and raised her hand in the air. Within seconds, a taxi pulled over, and in a moment, she had jumped into it and was gone.

Chapter 8

*D*evlin's mouth hung open in utter confusion. I looked

out the front window and clenched my teeth. If this was
not so uncomfortable, it might have been funny. The great
thing was, that now I would be free to drop off the
narcissist and get over to join my dad at the center.

Devlin searched the car for the ring, which he must have
found because he stopped crawling on the floor. I glanced
in the side mirror as he rubbed his chin where the huge
diamond had nicked him.

He got out of the car in a panther-like move, with his
phone in his hand. I could only assume he had dialed

Sofia, because even through the closed windows, I could hear him screaming.

I was bored with this charade. It was Christmas at the center, and I wanted to get home if this spoiled brat was done with his games.

He was fooling his father. What a jerk. Devlin had everything he ever wanted, and now he wanted his dad's company too. The only good thing was that he would most likely ruin the biz, and that would be karma at its best.

Somerset Industries was one of the top five businesses I wanted to see fail. They were the King of killing trees. Their box division was thriving—despite the ecological disaster brewing.

I sat quietly for another fifteen minutes until I couldn't take it anymore. "White Christmas" was on, and I was getting teary. Mr. I-Got-Dumped was in the back just sitting there staring out the window again. I rolled down the divider and cleared my throat.

"Mr. Somerset." I lowered my chauffeur's hat. "Where should I take you now?"

Devlin rumpled his dark hair in thought, and his gray eyes flashed. He glanced up at the female voice with curiosity and squinted his eyes.

"Where's Charles?"

I swallowed. "Ahh, he wasn't feeling well, so he sent me. I'm the best." I smiled winningly.

Everyone always said my smile was my best trait. Good teeth on my mother's side. I beamed that treasure at Devlin now, willing him to say, *Let's go home!*

He studied me. "How old are you? Are you even qualified to be a Rolls Royce limo driver?"

My face got warm, and I struggled to keep from swearing at him.

"I can assure you I am more than qualified. I grew up in the business."

Jerk off didn't have any clue *who* I was. Not that we had seen each other since we were children, but still, one thought he might put two and two together.

"I'll have to see your license."

I spun around and rolled the divider window down all the way. I'm sure I was anything but professional as I gripped him with my death-stare.

"Excuse me?" I said with all the disdain and professionalism I could muster together.

"Your license." He stuck the ring in his pocket and held out his hand for my documents.

I shook my head as I withdrew my backpack from under my seat and rummaged through it. I luckily found my ID. It wouldn't be the first time I'd left home without something I needed, just assuming it was in the mess of my bag somewhere.

I handed him my ID, and he took it and looked at it silently.

"Archer. You're Charles Archer's daughter?"

I nodded. Feeling defiant.

He handed back the ID and muttered. "I just have to be careful that you are who you say you are. Do you know how many women want to get close to the sexiest man of the year?"

I gurgled a half-laugh that came out as a snort. "Sorry. Allergies." I grabbed a tissue at the top of my purse and buried my face in it.

I had seen the cover of GQ and Devlin all over it with his handsome, rich, smug face. It had made me want to puke. How about naming someone the sexiest person that had contributed to the world and done something actually sexy–like inventing a machine to clear the plastic in the ocean or chaining themselves to a redwood to stop loggers? Something. Not just sitting in Daddy's office, keeping your pecks perfect and spending his money.

"Sexy is as sexy does," I said, for no good reason, except I assumed he was not smart enough to pick up on sarcasm.

I was wrong.

He looked up with a sneer that somehow made him even more handsome than his usual dumb-looking, charming Peter Pan look.

"Anyway, would you like me to take you home now?" I tried to keep the hope out of my voice.

He pulled the ring out of his pocket and looked at it wistfully. "No. I have to fix this somehow. I just have to think." He hit himself on the side of the head a little too hard.

I winced. Ouch.

More head hitting—this time harder.

"Hey—hey, stop that," I said. "You'll hurt yourself."

Devlin stopped like a child that had been reprimanded and stared at the ring again in a trance. Rich people problems. Maybe I should take him to his therapist.

"What, exactly, were you trying to get your fiancée to do?" I had to ask. "Because you obviously didn't want her to be herself."

Devlin threw his hands up. "She's beautiful."

I rolled my eyes.

"And?"

"Balderdash! I thought she was fine being single. Women!"

I looked at him with no sympathy.

He let out a big sigh. "My father's a traditionalist. I just thought it would be better this way. Make him happy. Win-win."

I shook my head.

"In what logical world did you think that you were going to bring home a porno star and get her to act like she was a perfect 50's wife?"

He clenched his hands.

"Right, I was crazy."

"Well, if you just needed a darn fake date, you would have been better off grabbing somebody off the street than trying to remake Sofia Denario!"

Devlin's gray eyes lit with a sparkle. "That's it! Great idea, great idea! I'll get a stand-in!" He beamed at me, and for a split second, just one, I could see why women swooned over him. Then he pushed the button, and the divider window rolled back up between us. Nothing like getting 'the hand' via a *window*—in case I had forgotten my station.

A half an hour later, we were still parked. Devlin had been on the phone nonstop. I continued to watch the snow come down hard and wondered when he'd give up and decide to go home.

I glanced back and saw him put his phone down for a minute, so I jumped at the moment. I had spotted a 7-Eleven across the street. At least I could ward off my boredom.

"Hey–" I rolled down the window and gestured to the glowing orb across the street. "I was going to run over to the store for a couple minutes, if that's okay?"

He raised dull eyes to me, lost in thought. "Sure. Whatever you want."

Even upset, he was good-looking. He didn't appear that much different from when he was five and he lost his favorite toy. I had seen his nanny look for hours one day because he was so distraught

Chapter 9

I walked back across the snowy street in my too-big

chauffeur uniform to the limo. Devlin seemed to be calling everyone on his contact list.

I turned on the radio and started listening and humming along to "Oh Holy Night" as I slurped my chocolate milk and finished off the last scratch off.

No luck.

As usual.

I stared out the window at the whiteout conditions. No other cars were on the road except emergency vehicles that skidded by with their lights blaring. The sky grew darker and more ominous, and I ushered away gloomy thoughts that were having a party in my head.

Two hundred thousand dollars.
Two hundred thousand dollars.

The most I'd won on a scratch-off was two hundred bucks, and I had been thrilled. This was a whole other level. Rich people money. Who the heck just has a hundred grand lying around, let alone two? Not anyone I knew.

Suddenly, I was struck motionless by a squealing banshee scream. It was Devlin. He was in the back, screaming. Yes, *screaming like a little girl watching a horror film.*

I rolled down the window. This was my chance to set another agenda.

"Are you okay? Would you like me to take you to a hospital? Or a bar?"

"No," he said angrily. Then screamed again, staring right at me.

I took a deep breath. How to mollify the little pansy in the back? I tried my go-to for narcissists.

"Well, *you look good.*"

He looked at me strangely, and then nodded thanks. "Do you think this cut will scar?"

I leaned in through the window closer to examine the tiny red dot left on his face from the engagement ring debacle.

I tried to act casually as the full impact of how handsome he truly was up-close hit me. And the smell. Rich smell, of course. Pine, deep hotness…

"I think it will be fine; no stitches needed. So, it's getting pretty gnarly out here…maybe we should go home—for our safety."

"Gnarly?" he mocked.

"Blizzard, hello?" I motioned to the whiteout around us.

He shook his head and pulled out a glass, pouring himself a shot of a deep golden liquid from a flask.

"I have no idea what to do. I am in a bad place right now."

This was getting beyond frustrating. My head was sweating under the cap, so I pulled it off and gave it some air, since we appeared to be going nowhere fast.

He looked at me differently—cocked his head to the side. His grey eyes bore into mine.

"Do I know you?"

I shook my head hoping he didn't remember running straight into me at the protest that afternoon.

"You have interesting eyes–you could almost be attractive if you wore some makeup and got out of that horrible uniform. Maybe got some highlights to offset that dirt color of your hair."

I sucked back a full sneer.

"Have you ever done any acting—what's your name, again?"

"Allie," I said roughly. "Allie Archer." I obviously did not impact him in my youth the way he had me.

"I took an acting class once as an undergrad. I was horrible; they let me play the elf. I'm working on my Master's in environmental science now."

He nodded. "That's great. Noble."

I tilted my head. "For the record, helping the environment is everyone's job, not just for the noble."

He looked up at me, more serious. I had that impact on people sometimes when I blurted out my desire to protect the world.

"You sound like the protestors we had removed today. You want to save the world *and* save jobs—you try it."

He shook his head and sipped on his cognac, looking like a model in a Ralph Lauren ad. Darn him.

"Anyway, it's getting late, and I'm in a very bad position. I have an unusual—but lucrative— proposition for you, most likely fueled by my current drunk and desperate situation."

He had my attention.

Lucrative was just what I happened to need.

He let out a deep breath. "I had planned to go home for Christmas to convince my father to resign and sign over all of the CEO duties to me. I've been handling all the day-to-day business anyway, but he's starting to…not be himself." He ran his hand through his dark hair and stared out the window.

"He's such a stubborn old coot." He laughed in spite of himself. "Well, his reasoning as to why he's reluctant to sign off is because I'm not ready. Not settled down…" His gray eyes met mine again.

"But Somerset Industries is in a bad place. I need to act now. We're losing profits hand over fist, and I'm fighting off a takeover by our competition—I need to be able to do business uninhibited so that I can save our family company."

For a moment, I related to him. I knew what it was like to want to save something so badly.

"I told him I was coming home with my fiancé so they could meet, and I hoped this would be the time he signed off for good and allowed me to take over. He's been grooming me his whole life." He looked down at the sparkling three-carat gem in his hand.

"As odd as this is, I have a proposal for you, Allie Archer."

My name dripped off his tongue like silver, and I felt myself blush like a schoolgirl. So not cool.

"If I pay you, will you pretend to be my fiancé for four days?"

He was serious.

I looked at him again.

"Who—me?"

He shrugged. "I can't find anyone else to do this at such short notice."

Oh, this was rich. Sure, just pay for me like a piece of cake you're picking up at a bakery. So typical! So rude!

"Just because I'm the hired help, you think you can make a proposition like that to me?"

"I have limited options, unfortunately, or I wouldn't ask. The last thing I can admit is that my 'exotic dancer' girlfriend left me because I won't commit."

Well, I would agree with him there. Still, my cheeks flamed. I had never had such a proposition in my life! One of those dim bulbs suddenly lit in my mind.

Hey–I had never had such a proposition in my life!

Devlin was still rolling the ring around in his hand and mumbling." Just tell me how much it'll cost; I'll make it worth your efforts…"

Instead of being irritated and insulted, the merest donning of an opportunity shone brightly. I took a breath and looked at him. Maybe this wasn't such a stupid idea after all.

He was desperate.
I was desperate.

Just earlier, I had been wishing and wishing on how to save the house. Who was I to question the way the universe brought it through? Maybe God had listened to my prayers for once. Here was my chance to help. Not pretty, for sure. Odd and uncomfortable, for certain. But It's not like I had to prostitute myself out, or…

I blurted out, "I don't have to–to touch you, do I?"

Devlin looked taken aback. "Well, not–not all the way, of course, but I'm going to need to hold your hand, maybe kiss…you know, it has to look real, like we're in love. You'll have your own room at night, no problem."

Hmmmm. Maybe we could make a deal that involved no broken legs or moral sins.

"Two hundred thousand dollars," I said flatly.

"Two hundred thousand dollars!" he echoed, outraged.

I tried to keep my face composed as if I bargained for two hundred thousand dollars every day. "Yeah, two hundred thousand dollars."

"Two hundred thousand dollars is ridiculous! I could get the best escort in New York for ten grand a night, and you're…"

I eyed him.

"*Here*," I said, "and your only option."
Devlin's eyebrows shot up together.
"Balderdash! Highway robbery."
"Maybe you could get an escort last minute at Christmas to lie to your whole family for four days. Or maybe not, since you've been calling people for the last hour and still don't have any options."
He looked up, incredulous. "You're serious? You want me to pay you two hundred thousand dollars?"
I stuck to my guns.
"I'm in a personal situation where I need two hundred thousand dollars, so yes, that's the price for four days of kissing and lying."
"You're impossible!"
"And you're a billionaire! What's the big deal? Stop being cheap. How bad do you want this?"
His gray eyes clouded.
"I'm not cheap."
"Then give me the two hundred thousand dollars to be your fake fiancé and let's go have a Merry Christmas!"

Chapter 10

$\mathcal{D}$evlin's eyes bore into mine.

"Fine. Two hundred thousand dollars. But I'm going to have to fix you up before I present you to my father. You need to *at least* seem worthy of having my children."

I remained silent.

To my credit.

Two hundred thousand dollars.

Before leaving town, he insisted we stop at an over-the-top, high-end shop on the Westside. They weren't open, but Devlin had called, and, like magic, a troop of attendants stood ready to help and the doors were opened.

I looked around, overwhelmed by the glitzy store filled with designer goods. I normally couldn't afford to walk in the front door of a place like this—now I was here in this bizarre *Pretty Woman* throwback, only instead of Richard Gere wanting to make me feel like a princess, Devlin seemed determined to kill the last smidgen of self-esteem I had.

He looked me up and down, as if seeing me for the first time. He examined every inch of my face, and then ran his glorious lash-fringed eyes down my frame bit by bit.

I swallowed uncomfortably.

He finally stopped and picked up a lock of my hair. "Seriously. You're a girl. Why would you ever let your hair be this–" he looked at my hair and shook his head in disgust—"boring?"

I glanced at the perfect retail crew, hoping they hadn't heard. I tugged my hair out of his fingers.

"I prefer natural."

"Please tell me you're not some crazy granola chick or something?"

"I like granola," I grunted defensively.

He pointed at my uniform. "I bet you have a *Save the World* T-shirt on under that attractive chauffeur outfit you're sporting." He laughed, and the retail army laughed back in a forced echo.

I wrapped my arms around myself. I did happen to be wearing my *Save the Trees* T-shirt, but I'd be darned if I'd tell him.

Humph. For somebody that was supposed to be charming, he certainly didn't seem to be using any of it on me.

Goodness knows you're not supposed to tell a girl her hair is mud-colored; that's insulting to anyone! It was true I hadn't bothered to do much with my hair lately, other than tying it in a ponytail for special occasions....

"I washed it yesterday." I defended myself instinctively, and felt it to see what kind of state it was in.

He looked doubtful. He continued clucking like a dissatisfied hen.

Darn Devlin Somerset. I obviously made a deal with the devil despite keeping my immortal soul intact. In any case, I wasn't about to let him see me flinch.

He addressed the staff. "So, let's get the little minion measured, and I'll consult with you on her wardrobe. We're also going to need a hairdresser to come in to have her hair dyed blonde, or nobody will ever believe that I dated her, let alone proposed."

I tried to contain the grimace on my face. I liked my earthy look, but he wanted glitz and a Beaver Cleaver clone. He was the worst of men.

A consultant was busy getting a hairdresser on the line when I heard Devlin whisper to her.

"Look, I know she's a cubic zirconia, but I need her to look like a diamond."

The stern-looking woman cast a shrinking look in my direction, as if I had personally failed all females. My hands balled up tight, and, although I've never hit anyone, I seriously could see how it happens.

He thinks he's too good for me?!

Fake hair, fake guy, fake morals! You want a fake? Oh, I can do fake. I can excel at a fake. Maybe not debutante level, but I could learn anything on YouTube.

Chapter 11

I couldn't wait to sneak away and tell my dad the good news about the money for the house. I stopped in my tracks when I had an upsetting thought. *Maybe I shouldn't say anything until I had the money in my hand.* I was suddenly unsure of how my dad might think of this. This could blow up in my face if I wasn't careful. This was *Devlin Somerset*–our biggest client. I didn't want to mess up in some way and cast a bad shadow on my father...

I glanced over at Devlin; he was considering some designer dresses. He looked so elegant and perfect and in shape. Sure, easy for him—he probably had nothing better to do all day than work on his body. Can't say it didn't appear to pay off in his having one heck of a physique.

Within minutes, I was whisked up by the salespeople and thrust into a room for measuring. To my horror, the staff whipped out tapes to analyze every inch of me. Speaking of horror, the back view I got of myself in my underwear was enough to send me running.

I was definitely going to have to add some kind of exercise to my routine. I liked to lie to myself and believe that carrying a protest sign to stop injustice might double as an arm exercise, but based on what I saw in the mirror, I was dead wrong. I didn't have much time to get upset over the state of my butt, either, because another group of people arrived like a buzzing beehive.

A manicurist.

A pedicurist.

And a hairdresser, complete with an assistant to carry her equipment.

After what seemed like hours of being abused with bleach and stupid talk, Devlin emerged into the backroom to check me out. My hair had been stripped, beaten, and dyed nearly white blonde. I looked like a fright night bride.

He smiled. "Now that looks like a girl I might date—at least briefly."

I really wanted to punch him, I really did, but the cruel hairdressing wench still had my locks clenched in a brush/blow dryer combo, so I couldn't reach him.

I shouted over the dryer.

"Do you know how upsetting this is to me as a woman, that just because I put some blonde in my hair, you now find me attractive?"

Devlin smiled and shrugged, but didn't' apologize.

Soon, the retail people were smiling ear to ear, full of Somerset cash and ready to get home to their families as they loaded all the clothes Devlin had picked out for me into the back of the Rolls Royce limo.

He looked me over, with my new platinum hair and expertly applied makeup, and nodded his head as if I passed some man examination.

"Let's see the nails."

I gritted my teeth and held out my hands that now sported long French manicured, perfect nails. I awaited the Prince's approval.

He nodded and pulled something from his pocket.

It was Sofia's diamond ring.

I stared at the intense sparkles that bounced and beamed all around us. The ring must be worth a fortune. I had never seen anything so obscene. I loved it. So much for not being materialistic.

"You're going to have to put the ring on. I hope it fits." With that, he slipped it on my left hand. It fit as perfect as Cinderella's glass slipper.

We both looked down silently at the ring on my wedding finger, and *just like that, I was engaged to Devlin Somerset.*

Chapter 12

"You can drive me as usual, in the proper attire for a chauffeur, and as befitting your station. We will change you into a proper dress when we get closer to Kissing Bridge," said Devlin. "You can leave the hat off, so you don't get that matted hair thing you had going."

I turned and tight smiled at him. "Just to be clear. You're sounding a bit condescending to me–may I remind you that your other option was a stripper? *And that she's not an option?*"

Devlin settled in and helped himself to a glass of cognac. He checked his watch.

"Behind schedule, but disaster averted. We should be there in four hours or so."

He rolled up the divider window between us and I started the limo and kept my eyes focused on the road. I heard him pour himself another glass and the ice cubes hit the crystal as they clunked in. The back-speaker button buzzed on.

"Listen. I–I feel like we got off to the wrong start," he said through the speaker. "I know we are faking this, but we…have to be believable. My family is…difficult."

I almost felt some sympathy. Maybe I had been kind of harsh. I sighed.

"Don't worry. I love family gatherings," I replied. "I'm great with old people, kids, spoiled brats…" I glanced in the rearview mirror.

I felt transfixed by the way his chiseled jaw was somehow made even more glorious by the thin red scratch that the thrown ring had left. Like a mole on Cindy Crawford's mouth. Figures.

He looked up and caught me staring at him, and I fell into those deep puddles of gray. Gray into blue, endless and forever…

"Listen, just don't fall for me, okay?" he said matter-of-factly. "I can't deal with the extra drama. This is a business deal."

I sucked back a full laugh, but it came out like a gurgle. I cast my eyes to the road and hoped he didn't see my flaming face.

How dare he. That said, I couldn't be sure my face
hadn't resembled some swooning teenager. Gosh, I was
horrible with men! I was equally ignorant around the men I
loved and the men I abhorred. Ugh. I felt like sticking my
tongue out at him, but thankfully controlled myself and
arranged my face to look like I was at a job interview.
Which, in some respects, I was.

"I can assure you that won't be a problem, Mr.
Somerset," I said professionally.

He looked at me in that mind-blowing intense way, and I
felt my heart being sucked out like from a Dementor's kiss.

"Okay. And it's Devlin. Or honey, or…" He made a
motion to roll down the window between us, and then
stuck his perfectly chiseled face through the divider.

"Okay, honey." He fingered a lock of my fake white hair.
"Suits you."

I raised my chin and tried to ignore how ungodly manly
he was. He certainly was proud of his handiwork. I glanced
in the mirror.

Bridezilla.

And he liked it. Men were idiots over blondes, and this
playboy was no different.

I smiled as the traffic light changed green, and I hit the
gas, thinking of ways to torture him that still included me
getting that two hundred thousand.

Chapter 13

I drove the limo, and Devlin continued drinking and filling me in on his life story.

He started getting wistful and mopey when he brought up the old Long Island estate. Its glory days had faded with the new millennium.

"It just never was the same after…" He stopped talking and concentrated on pouring more golden liquor from the canister into his crystal glass.

I glanced back to see him looking as if he might cry.

"I remember you back then when your family still kept all the cars there," I said. "I was a little girl, and I thought you were a real-life prince. Your hair was blonde then, and it glowed like the sun."

He looked up and smiled lazily. "Yeah, weird I was a toe head. Not anymore." He ran his hand through his thick dark hair, and I found it hard to focus on the road. He caught my eyes in the rearview mirror.

"And you–you were a young girl who hid when I looked your way."

I blushed.

"You were a good hider; you were very small– little. Well, you're still little."

I bit my lip. I couldn't argue with that.

"And you're all grown up now. Good for you." He raised his glass in congratulations.

"Thanks," I said, for lack of anything witty to add.

But for some reason, I went on. "We didn't live there long, but I do remember one year you had a grand ball for Christmas. My father let me stay up and watch all the cars arriving and all the beautiful couples."

He glanced up at me with a sad look. "My mother always organized it…"

He cleared his throat.

"You moved out when your dad wanted to start his own car business," Devlin continued.

I snorted a gross, embarrassing nose sound. The truth was, his older sister, Sissy Somerset, had taken up painting and demanded our home for her new art studio. Mom had recently been diagnosed, and being asked to move was the worst timing ever.

In the end, we managed to find a new home, but the extra stress on Mom and Dad had been so hard to witness. As a child, I had felt so weak and unable to do anything. But now, I was a grown woman. I wasn't about to pretend.

"Ah, not quite," I corrected him in my schoolteacher's tone. Just the facts ma'am. I clenched the wheel tighter.

"What you mean to say is that your sister wanted our apartment for her art studio, so we were told to move."

Devlin's eyes bore into mine, and one aristocratic brow rose in understanding. I turned my eyes back to the road.

"Humph," Devlin said. "Well, I'm the youngest, so they always gilded the lily with me. I should have guessed. Balderdash, really. She's horrible that way. Whatever Sissy wants, Sissy gets. She took my pet pony."

"What?" I was taken aback.

"It's true. It was a gift from my grandmamma too. She talked our mother into believing that I was too young and irresponsible. A running stereotype, I might add." He flashed a dazzle of brilliant white, and I shielded my eyes. How did a person get their teeth that bright?

"We had an entire staff at the stables to tend to the pony, not to mention all the other horses. But no matter. Sissy got her way in the end. My dear pony, Duke, became *Teacup*." He stared out the window, forlornly recalling his trauma.

I rolled my eyes to myself.

It was hard to have sympathy for his spoiled rich people problems. *My sister took my pony oh, waaaaa.* Try keeping food on the table on the wage you paid your employees. I shook my head. They might have money, but those Somersets were still deranged. At least they could afford therapists.

Devlin leaned forward through the divider suddenly, and my pulse quickened. He cocked his head.

"But my family did *invest* in your dad's current business, didn't he?"

I looked at him uncomfortably with his man-ness so close to me. It was true. Mr. Harold Somerset II had in fact given Dad the seed money to start Archer Premier Transport. I had forgotten that.

"Yes, he did. We're very grateful for that. I look forward to seeing your father. He was always very kind to me. He brought me chocolate milk."

I smiled.

Devlin's brow rose. "I wasn't allowed to drink chocolate milk."

I shrugged. "He obviously liked me better."

He laughed in spite of himself, and it made me glow with a nice, warm feeling.

"In any case, I don't think he'll remember you—according to my sister, he's forgetting more and more every day. I should think it best we just don't mention any prior associations–so as not to confuse him."

I pursed my lips. "Sure, anything you want."

****

I pumped the gas into the limo, and Devlin came out of the convenience store with a new bottle of cognac.

He watched me as I hovered over the gasoline pump. Snowflakes fell on his broad shoulders, and the lamppost haloed his handsome face.

I focused back on the pumping. "Let's talk about what we should know if we really knew each other well as lovers do…" I said professionally.

"Honey…" He teased, and his mouth screwed up in a cute, tipsy slant.

Devlin hovered over me, too close, blowing on his hands.

"So, what would be your favorite meal for me to cook– honey?" I joked.

"We have chefs for that," Devlin said as he opened the bottle and took a big swig. I looked around uneasily.

Good grief, did rich people think they were above the law? My friend drank one beer at the boardwalk and got a three-hundred-dollar ticket. Truth be told, we were in the middle of nowhere, and we seemed to be the only idiots out in the inclement weather.

"Are you sure you should be drinking? I thought you were trying to impress your father."

"Look, my dad isn't doing so well right now. He certainly won't notice me drinking. I rarely drink, by the way. I'm stress drinking."

I made a face. I could understand that. I stress drank chocolate milk.

I grabbed the squeegee thing and wiped at the dirt and snow stuck on the Rolls' window. We had entered the foothills of the Vermont Mountains and I needed to be able to see as clearly as possible.

"Well, if I was your *real-life fiancé*... I would be doing the cooking. I think it's artistic—my dad taught me."

He studied me.

"You're serious."

"Yes. I love to cook; it's a labor of love!"

He laughed. "You certainly are different from my other girlfriends." He toasted me with his expensive bottle and took another slug.

"I doubt you can cook as well as our three-star Michelin chef Pierre, though."

I grunted. "I probably can't cook as well as a three-star Michelin chef. Okay, moving on. Favorite color?"

"Blue," he fired back.

"Okay, mine is orange."

Devlin nodded. "Got it."

"Favorite city?" I asked.

"Monte Carlo." He snapped his fingers as if he had answered correctly on a game show. "Great bars, great beaches."

"For me, it would be Buffalo."

"Buffalo? New York? Balderdash! Why?"

"Have you seen Niagara Falls?! It's amazing, and the Great Lakes…nobody knows how awesome they are if they haven't been there in the summer."

Devlin rolled his eyes. "Have you ever been out of the country?"

"No—but someday, I want to visit the Amazon."

"Good malaria grief, whatever for?"

"The rainforest. It's getting torn down; I want to see it and help protect it. It's being burned, and…"

Devlin took a big sip with a warning glance at me. Then sauntered back to the limo door and waited.

I bit my tongue and went over to open the door for him. His breath was hot next to me.

"I'm never going to remember this shallow chat, you know. Just go along with everything I say and, if in doubt, just kiss me."

My eyebrows rose.

"Excuse me?" I said, turning around. "Kiss you?"

He waved away my alarm with a flick of his wrist. "Yes, kiss me. I don't have time to memorize your life—we're not on the newlywed game, were here to get my father to do one thing: sign the business over to me so I can save our family's legacy."

Before I knew it, his lips were on mine, and I was lifted into the closest thing to heaven I could remember. I didn't even mind that I wasn't breathing when he stopped and looked at me triumphantly.

"Good. I just wanted to get that out of the way so we could get the act right."

I came back to my senses quickly and hated him again.

Suddenly, his eyes narrowed, and he leaned in. I backed up in case he was going to surprise-kiss me again.

"You!" he pointed a finger at my face. "I recognize your face now."

I scrunched up said face.

"The protester."

"The polluter," I spat back.

"Ahaaa."

"Just get in the car," I said, holding the limo door open. He sneered but slid in.

Chapter 14

*D*evlin was asleep in the back, and I was happy to have time to think. I had thought that pulling off this ruse would be easy.

I glanced at my phone. Dad would be in the middle of handing out presents right now. I was so happy he could be there. I sent off a quick text to him: *Change of plans – going to Vermont for four days to escort Devlin home to see his father. Everything great here. Will be home for Christmas with a big surprise. Don't worry and don't forget to send pictures ho ho ho.*

I hoped I wouldn't mess this up somehow. If all went well, I would have the best Christmas surprise for my father ever—even if it looked like I wouldn't be home to share it with him.

At a stop sign, I pulled up some etiquette tutorials on YouTube and let it play as I drove–it began with forks and glass placement at a proper table and moved to correct posture and appropriate conversation.

I made a face when I heard the old cliché *don't talk about politics or religion.* This was why nothing ever changed for the better, because good people in decent society weren't supposed to talk about anything ugly. How did we change anything if we don't all talk about the issues?

This one would be hard for me. Especially since getting a chance to lecture the Somersets about fair wages and protecting the environment was a dream come true. Better than a protest outside of their windows.

I continued to drive up the sleek and slippery road filled with snow. I could barely see, and we were moving at a slug's pace. Plus, I was hungry. I checked my map app. Looked like another hour up the hill to Kissing Bridge Mountain where the Somersets had their ski chalet.

After what seemed a nightmarish eternity driving through blinding white, I spotted twinkling welcoming lights in the distance and pulled into a small central town.

A café glittered all cozy and warm; it looked inviting with smoke puffing from the rooftop. Devlin was still deep asleep in the back. I considered leaving him, but then maybe he'd freeze, and I'd never get the two hundred thousand dollars.

I reached over and shook him gently. "Devlin," I said lightly. He looked so vulnerable and handsome asleep. But even my best friend's evil children looked like angels when they slept.

He definitely was one hot angel. I pulled my eyes away.

The warm glow from the window and the faint aroma of something delicious floated out of the café. The sign above read *Landers' Bakery, Blue Ribbon Winners of Vermont.*

I grabbed a sweater from my backpack and draped it over Devlin. I had to go in. It was too tempting, and I was tired of driving. My stomach rumbled. Was it only eight hours ago that Dad and I had shared goulash in the kitchen and wished for a miracle? It seemed like a lifetime away.

Devlin was snoring like a little kitten, and I smirked and shut the limo door softly. I would just head in for a minute and grab something to go.

Chapter 15

*T*he Lander's Bakery was an oasis in my nightmare. It was cabin style and quaint with a bubbling clientele and windows filled with baked goods.

I hustled to get in line at the bakery counter. I had my eye on the cinnamon bun as big as my foot. I could taste it already.

"Hey!" came the irritating call behind me.

I turned to see Devlin striding through the door. Some customers called out to him, and he softened and waved back. He seemed to know many of the people in there. He was by my side in a moment.

"What, did you think you were going to let me freeze in the Rolls and then pawn the ring for your money?" he hissed in my ear.

My mouth fell open, and he reached over and snapped it shut–which of course made me even more furious.

The tension was broken by a rambunctious senior with a towering red beehive that came barreling over and wrapped her arms around both of us.

"Devlin, dear, it's been so long!" She smiled, and her light blue eyes sparkled when she looked at me.

"And you must be...."

Devlin sucked in his breath and grabbed my hand. "My fiancé, actually."

The senior's eyes crinkled up so they were barely visible. "Well, well, what wonderful news! So, we should be expecting a wedding up at the house soon?"

I gulped, and Devlin grinned his easy fake smile that didn't reach his eyes. "Well, one step at a time, Carol. This is Allie. Allie, this is the infamous Carol Landers. She and her sister, Ethel, have put all the other bakers out of business."

"Not so! Now, don't be spreading falsehoods, Devlin." A petite silver-haired lady came forth, taking off her apron.

She stuck out her hand to me. "Ethel Landers. And we've only out-won everyone, not put them out of business."

"Correct!" her feisty bee-hived sister said. And then they both started laughing.

Devlin beamed. I could see he had genuine affection for this quirky duo.

"I heard you opened up a full restaurant–we could use dinner; it's been a long drive."

Ethel brightened. "Yes, our new *Enchanted Café*!" She hooked her arm through mine. "Just this way, through the red connecting doors."

I looked back wistfully at the cinnamon roll I had had my heart set on joined by a glass of chocolate milk. Oh well.

Ethel whispered in my ear, "Don't worry. I'll make sure you leave with some baked goods." I smiled, and she winked at me.

Soon we were seated at an elegant white table with beautiful silver, and china plates. The full moon had slid out of the cloud cover, and now it lit up the mountains of Kissing Bridge through the picture window.

Tiny Christmas lights twinkled, hanging from the wood beams and creating a fairy wonderland. I had never been up to a ski town, and I was charmed. Everyone was so friendly, and the food smelled amazing. My stomach made a low growl, and I looked up to see Devlin glaring at me.

I leaned in. "I wasn't trying to let you freeze. I was just going to grab a pastry."

His scalding look said he didn't believe me.
I grabbed a roll and focused on applying some butter.

"Let's get on to other things. We have some elegant events in the next couple of days, and we need to talk about etiquette."

I wasn't about to tell him I'd been binge-watching etiquette YouTube for that very reason. "Your alternative was an exotic dancer," I reminded him.

Devlin looked over the wine menu.

"Her mother was a Baroness. She went to the best finishing school."

I looked down at the forks. I had this one covered, as there was only one of everything. I flicked my napkin open and wove it about like a flag and dramatically draped it on my lap and went back to buttering my roll.

"Like that." Devlin flicked his hand without lifting his gaze from the wine menu.

I looked at my roll. Was eating carbs considered lousy etiquette now? Possibly we lived in a new gluten-free world, and I hadn't been apprised of it.

He looked over at my bread plate. "You don't dip your knife into the universal butter and reuse it. You scoop some butter onto your plate, and *then* you transfer it to the bread from your plate."

This was so exasperating! How the heck could I learn every nuance of fine society in such a short time, no matter how much I crammed? It was all so frivolous and stupid and rich people problems. I let out an irritated huff.

"And don't huff and grumble like you're on a chain gang."

"Seriously, do you know how many trees they are cutting down in the rainforest? Abusing the natural resources and driving the indigenous tribes and animals out? Real-world problems, Devlin! Not your fancy-dancy pants SHALLOW life issues! *Use this fork, don't' drink chocolate milk, don't spit.* Where does it end?"

"Okay, that's what I'm talking about," he drawled as he leaned back in his chair.

"What?" I said as I put the butter on my plate and stuck my tongue out at him.

"You—you ranting and raving about saving the world. Nobody cares. It's boring."

My mouth hung open.

"And that is completely unattractive!"

He snapped my chin shut, and my teeth clicked.

RUDE! I fixed him with my full Betty Boop I-mean-business glare.

"It's called giving a darn. I wish more people with your money did. It would be world-changing."

He laughed.

"And what would you do with the money—give it all away and buy the rainforest?"

"Yes!" I declared. "I'd buy it to protect it, yes. Someone has to. It's a resource, and they sell it for cattle or palm oil; why not for a protected world park?"

He motioned the server over. "As I was saying. Let's stay away from *volatile* subjects, or anything that might lead my father or whomever to ask questions about us. Like the date of our wedding, etc."

"So, what can I talk about?"

He looked out the window and gestured.

"The weather."

"The weather?" My mouth curled up. "You want me to prattle on about the weather? What's to say? It's snowing. Oh, looks like snow. *Hey, snow again what do you know?*"

Devlin faced me. "How about you just *don't talk at all.* Fine ladies often just sit and look good. Can't go wrong."

"Really? Seriously?" I arched a brow and shook my head.

Devlin was all smiles as he ordered the wine. It fell as soon as she left, and he leaned over and hissed at me again.

"Look, I'm paying you. Can you just act like a good employee? I'm not asking you to do anything *except keep your mouth shut.* Have wine, of course. But zip it!" He made the zipper motion across his mouth and dead-eyed me.

I shook my head. He'd obviously never seen me after two glasses of wine, or he'd know keeping my mouth shut after that was no option.

Everything inside me felt worthless. We were a foot away, but worlds apart. Devlin was right. I just needed to do my job and get out with the money. But why did part of me want to teach Mr. Fancy Pants a lesson?

My mouth must have been hanging agape again after the last insult, and Devlin instinctively reached over and tapped me under the chin to close it. Again.

I didn't like this pattern that was forming. "I'd appreciate if you didn't finger my face," I snapped.

Devlin almost spit out his wine.

Suddenly, the sun emerged, and he smiled from ear to ear. "My nanny used to do that to me, and I hated it too. Sorry, old habits die hard and all that…"

I looked up at him from under my fake lashes. Was that an apology? He must be getting drunk. He sure looked good drunk, I had to admit. Somehow, the inebriation just brought out a more easy-going charm that had remained hidden before.

Now, he was adorable with his childlike grin, even while he hurled insults at me. Still, he was Devlin, and I hated him. I wasn't about to get my plans waylaid by some hot guy.

Ethel Landers came over and uncorked a new bottle. Devlin winked at her and pulled over a glass, filling it with some wine.

He pushed it toward me. "Drink."

I wasn't too sure about this. We needed to be on our wits. I wasn't about to come this close to getting my two hundred grand and have it fail.

"To us."

I smiled.

"Darling."

He laughed again. "You might be common, but you're funny."

Ugh. He had to go and ruin it.

Chapter 16

*D*evlin was twirling his wine around in the glass and looking like little Lord Fauntleroy in his perfectly tailored Gucci suit. He made it seem so effortless.

I nibbled daintily on the blueberry crumble we had for dessert. Typically, I would have ordered a chocolate milk and extra whipped cream, but I refrained.

Devlin looked me up and down.

"We'll leave the limo at the car rental down the street and pick up something more suitable. I can't have my fiancé driving me."

I nodded and rolled up my uniform sleeve that had fallen into the whipped cream.

Devlin looked at me with a glint of disgust.

"What?" I said, swiping a piece of crumble from the corner of my mouth.

"Slow down. You look like you haven't eaten in a month."

"Well, this is the best blueberry crumble I've ever had."

He looked at me with the side of his mouth pulled down. "Better change here as well before we drive up. I don't expect my father to still be awake this late, but just in case."

I nodded as I finished up the last of my dessert. The sister with the flaming beehive appeared with a coffee pot in hand.

"Did you like it?" she asked me.

"Oh, yes! So unique!" I smiled.

"It's our special recipe."

"Yum! It's extraordinary, indeed. I couldn't place the one spice you had in there–"

The elderly lady laughed a sweet, deep belly sound. "It's not often I get to serve up the *Marry Me Blueberry Crumble*. But we slipped it in on our manager, Kat, so we had some extra leftover." She leaned over and brought her finger to her mouth. "Mums the word." She winked at me like I was Bonnie to her Clyde.

Devlin took one delicate bite and nodded his head. "Truly superb–as usual. What kind of crumble did you say this was?"

She refilled our coffee and smiled.

"*Marry Me Blueberry Crumble.*"

I gulped. "I never heard of that."

She clapped me on the back. "That's because we only serve it to people that wanted to get married. Can't be messing with those single people! Ha-ha."

"Marriage? I almost spit up my coffee when I caught Devlin shaking his head at me.

"What?"

"You're engaged, right?"

I nodded and recovered.

"Yes–I just adore him."

Devlin gave a tight smile.

"Well, then–no harm is done." She beamed.

I turned to Devlin, who looked amused at my discomfort.

"Better be careful–I've seen some mighty strange magic come out of this place." He was enjoying my unease.

I blushed. Obviously, they were joking with me—making the new girl the butt of their joke.

Chapter 17

*D*evlin rented a truck, and we left the Rolls at the rental place. He opened the passenger door for me, and I knew things were about to get real.

He drove with expertise up the mountain roads. I hadn't expected him to know how to drive, let alone handle himself on icy terrain.

"Okay, so our 'falling in love at first sight' story– how's that going to go?" Devlin asked.

I thought about it. "People fall in love quickly sometimes. It makes sense. We need a good story."

Devlin looked doubtful, but waved for me to continue. "Such as…?"

I wracked my brains for memories of all the syrupy Hallmark films I binged-watched. They all had adorable first meetings—none I could remember on the spot.

"We have so much to lie about. Maybe we can keep as much truth as possible. What if I actually did pick you up for a ride, and you took one look at me and knew I was the one."

Devlin smirked at me. "There is no way I'm letting my father know who you really are."

I guessed he was right. Better keep it as simple as possible.

"Let's just say we met at the horse races?" he offered.

I frowned. "How about a protest rally?"

He snorted.

"Let's settle on a bar. You were hovering at the VIP section begging to get in, and I saw you and decided–you were the one."

He glanced at me; I shook my head.

"Fine. Just stick to saying as little as possible and let me answer the questions if in doubt."

"What about all this snow we're having?" I said like a Stepford wife.

He looked at me with a dangerous glint in his eye. "Just don't talk, please. Easiest money you'll ever make."

I nodded. Not that I had a choice.

Still. I was going to have to step up my game to make his father believe the chauffeur's daughter had whisked his commitment-phobic son off the market.

CHAPTER 18

*T*he Chalet, or should I say *mansion*, in the mountains
was epic. Luxurious on a whole other level. All those
shows where you see the super-rich houses…yeah, those
aren't the REALLY rich ones. The super-rich people hide
their stuff. The real rich are sequestered behind huge
bushes or long driveways or up high in the mountains like
this.

   I felt my mouth gaping and closed it before Devlin
reprimanded me.

 An older man in a fancy, formal uniform answered the
door and beamed.

   "Mr. Devlin, sir! What a surprise, sir, you made it."

   Devlin grabbed both his hands. "Jeeves, how great to
see you."

"You too sir, truly. Your father has retired, but he will be thrilled you came home."

I hesitated a few feet behind Devlin. He held out his hand to me, and I stepped forward carefully on my ridiculously high heels.

"Jeeves, this is Allie. My fiancé."

Jeeves's eyebrows rose, and he bent from the waist in a deep bow. "My honor to meet you, Miss Allie." He kissed my hand.

"Me, too," I mumbled, and threw in a weird curtsy.

"Jeeves is my father's butler and one of my favorite people." The elder Jeeves blushed.
He cleared his throat.

"I'll have James get your luggage, sir, and if you give me a moment, I'll have Alice freshen up your room."

Devlin ushered me into the mansion, and I tried not to gawk. It looked like something out of Downton Abbey.

"Miss Allie will be needing her own room—" Devlin said. "She snores horribly."

I blushed.

"Let's put her in the South Wing—The Sapphire Room."

Jeeves glanced about uncomfortably. "I'm sorry, sir, but all the rooms are taken."

Devlin spun around. "What are you talking about? This place has more than a dozen rooms."

Jeeves's mouth went tight, and he rang a bell. A young red-haired woman appeared in full French maid garb. Black uniform with a frilly white apron.

"Please have Mr. Devlin's room straightened up, and remove the dogs…"

Devlin's eyes bulged. "Dogs? Jeeves, you know full well I'm allergic to dogs. What in the world could have possessed you?"

A look of dawning came over him, and he went deadly silent.

"She's here."

Jeeves nodded.

"Balderdash!" Devlin exploded. "She brought those prize poodles across the country?"

Devlin looked angrier than I had ever seen. He spat out, "Sissy."

"Yes, sir," Jeeves said. "With the entire family and her maid and nanny. That's why we don't have any spare rooms. She insisted the children each have their own suite, and the baby…"

I cocked my head. Sounded like the same old spoiled Sissy.

"Just get the poodles out of our room. It's been a long night, and we're going to bed."

My heart wiggled at the 'our room' comment. That was, hopefully, a mistake. I struggled to look calm and relaxed when Jeeves helped Devlin off with his coat. "I did reject the idea of the dogs going in your room, sir, quite demonstratively, but she insisted you weren't coming, again…"

He trailed off and looked chagrined.

Devlin patted him on the back. "Not your fault, good man. I know my sister is impossible to say no to."

"Yes, sir." He hung up Devlin's coat. I took mine off and hobbled over to hang it up when I saw Devlin giving me the evil eye in my periphery. I stopped in my tracks.

Jeeves turned and smiled and took my coat from me. "Allow me, Miss Allie."

—

Chapter 19

*T*he hallways upstairs were elaborate. The carpet was a

deep red with golden scrolls like a fancy casino. The ceiling boasted bold, rustic logs with grandiose crystal, brilliant chandeliers hanging from them.

The young maid, Alice, came bustling out of the end room with sheets under her arm, and in her hand the leashes of two extremely large, matching white poodles. They pulled and yanked her forward as she attempted to close the door behind her.

Devlin took out a handkerchief and held it over his mouth. The dogs suddenly lurched forward and broke free from the overwhelmed maid and barreled straight toward us. They both leaped on me and began pawing and drooling all over my new dress. Did I mention dogs love me?

I love dogs, too, but drool and Chanel is not a good match. It's one thing to be in jeans and a T-shirt— no problem. T-shirts are made for dogs and dirt and real work.

I looked down at myself, and I had gobs of poodle spittle splotched all over my first designer duds. I gave in and petted the dogs anyway. Dogs will be dogs.

Devlin finally pulled them off of me, aided by the maid. "So sorry, miss. So sorry, Mr. Devlin."

He tugged me into the safety of the room and shut the door.

Chapter 20

𝒟ark, ornate furniture accompanied a fire crackling in
the corner. Devlin plopped down on the massive bed that
was covered with a festive red quilt and ran his hands
through his hair. I couldn't help but think he looked like a
model in one of those Halston cologne commercials. I
wonder if he knew that move had that effect, and that's
why he did it.

  I cast my eyes away from his Siren's song. Instead, I
looked around the comfortable room and realized I wasn't
in Kansas anymore. I had never seen this kind of splendor.
Ski chalet, ha! Royal Palace in the snow was more like it.

For the first time, the realization of how a billionaire lived was my reality.

"This changes everything," Devlin croaked, as he looked up at me from under those long lashes. "I had no idea the General would be here."Devlin got up and began pacing back and forth.

"We need to get ready for a nuclear strike."

"Excuse me?"

"My sister and her entire family...this is a whole other level of fraud."

He studied me. "She can't recognize you. She can't know this is a stunt, or this will backfire on me—and you."

Sissy had always been such a princess, so I wasn't thrilled about her being there either. I didn't even have sibling rivalry weirdness going for me.

Devlin was right. I wasn't sure what kind of wrench her knowing me might throw into the picture. Surely, she had seen the papers and knew the truth about Devlin's girlfriend. How would we explain that?

Gosh, darn it. I couldn't figure this out. I didn't get my doctorate in science or anything; I'm just trying to save the world.

Devlin was bent on wearing a hole in the pricey Persian rug as he continued to pace back and forth like a panther. It kind of turned me on, for some reason.

He was beside himself ranting and huffing as he strode back and forth, tossing his glorious hair around him like some rakish romance hero.

"This is never going to work. We should just turn around and go back to Manhattan and forget everything."

Yes, yes! The inside of me screamed. *Let's get out of this bedroom, off this blizzard mountain, and get home so I can spend Christmas with my dad and celebrate saving the house with my –*

"Hey, wait–what about my two hundred thousand dollars?" I cried.

He stopped pacing.

"You can't expect me to pay you for an unfinished job."

"That's not my fault."

"I'll pay you double your rate for the car service–let's go."

My Christmas miracle was falling apart.

"NO! We had a deal. I thought you were a businessman. You can't just go and renege on your word. I watch crime shows! We had a verbal agreement, which is binding in court, I might add!" Well, I think.

"Fine. I'll pay you triple." He checked his watch.

"I may get home in time for the after-hours VIP party at the Ritz. Come on, I'll have Jeeves bring our things back down…"

"Wait," I said as I jumped up and grabbed his arm.

"Look at this." I pointed to my face and hair.

"You did this to me. Disfigured me into some sort of Pygmalion blonde clone!"

"And? You should *thank* me!" He snapped his fingers. "Plus, we need to deduct the clothes."

I stamped my foot. "That I don't want?! How are you going to convince your dad you're a man of your word when you can't even keep one promise? I'm deformed. You're paying anyway."

He put his hands on his hips.

"Make me."

I put my hands on my hips back.

"Don't threaten me. I have a YouTube following, Devlin Somerset."

Devlin threw his hands up. "Ooooh, frightening. How many views do you get, fifteen?"

I squished my lips together. My YouTube channel had not flourished as I had hoped, but I had thirty dedicated fans and growing.

I had to think quickly. "Look, your sister is here for the holidays all the way from Los Angeles."

"Don't remind me."

"And why do you think she's here?"

A light flickered in his gray eyes as realization dawned.

"She wants something from Dad."

I nodded. "Bingo." I did his finger snap thing back at him, although my snap is lame. Not all clear and commanding like his. "If you go home now, who knows

what she'll talk your father into? You said he's not well and
you haven't seen him in five years?"

"Right."

"That's unforgivable, I might add, not seeing your father
for that many years." I shook my head.

"I've been running the company. It's what he wanted."

I dead-eyed him. "We need to do this! You worked
hard, you earned it, right?"

He nodded. "Every day for the last five years, I've lived
and breathed it. I had hoped he'd be proud of me."
He let out a long breath and looked chagrined. "Seems
despite my dedication and the business flourishing, old
stereotypes die hard. Which is why I concocted this whole
stupid charade to begin with."

I put my hands on his shoulders; it was a reach. "That is
exactly why you need to show him how well-adjusted you
are with your loving fiancé!"

He looked down at me with an uncertain slump.

"Come on," I urged, like I was a coach trying to get him
to score. "When the going gets tough, the tough get
going. You're not going to let your sister win, are you?"

He shook his head.

"This better work, or we're both screwed. If Sissy figures
out our game, the collateral damage could get ugly. Are
you prepared?"

Fear gripped me like a tightening noose. There was no
going back now. I nodded with as much enthusiasm as I
could muster.

"And good grief, whatever happens, she can't know you are our chauffeur's daughter!"

I gulped.

Chapter 21

*D*evlin continued to gaze into the fire, lost in thought.

But I was exhausted. I looked around the room, hoping there was some connected suite with a bed for me that I wasn't seeing. Sadly, as big as the place was, there was only one huge bed. I rubbed my neck.

"Um, there is only one bed," I mumbled.

He glanced around the room absently. "You can take the couch; it's comfortable."

My mouth hung open. How rude. He looked as if he were ready to do the chin-click thing, so I shut it quickly and eyed him.

"Well, *as your fiancé,* don't you think that the love of your life should be comfortable? I'm sure you meant *you* were offering to sleep on the couch?"

He looked at me.

"Are you a virgin, or just horrible with men?"

I nearly spit out my indignity.

"Um, what does that have to do with anything?" He was, if possible, more offensive than earlier.

Oooh, I hated him.

Here he was, all upset over his rich person's problems, while my father and I fought to save our two-bedroom home in Jersey. If he thought I was going to feel bad for him, he could think again.

He waved his hand at the bed. "This bed is as large as a polo field; I had it designed myself. I could barely locate you in it if I wanted too. I'll take one side. You take the other."

I swallowed. I wasn't about to be delegated like a servant to sleep at the settee at his feet.

And Mr. Rude wasn't doing the very chivalrous thing, according to YouTube's etiquette rules.

"Fine. But I'm putting up a pillow wall for propriety's sake. Just stay on your side."

He scrunched his face up. "The least of your worries."

He looked lost in thought, and I didn't care to delve into his narcissistic issues. *Oh, the poodles were in my room—ghastly. Oh, my sister came home at the same time—how will I cope?*

Try buying scratch-offs hoping you can get college book money.

There was a knock at the door, and Jeeves entered with silver tray, champagne, and strawberries. He was followed by a thin man with bifocals wearing a formal uniform and pushing our suitcases.

Devlin took a glass and went over to mope by the fire. Now he looked like another Ralph Lauren ad. Darn him and his good looks.

"Thank you!" I said, reaching in my purse for some tip money.

Devlin's hand grabbed mine mid-motion as I removed my wallet.

"That will be all, Jeeves."

The two servants nodded and retreated. This was uncomfortable, to say the least. Devlin drank and stared at the fire. I could feel his urge for flight.

I poured myself a glass of champagne, since he didn't offer, and went into the bathroom to change. He might need to sit up and brood all night, but I was exhausted, and I wanted to talk to Dad and check-in.

I finally located a nightgown that looked like something Zsa Zsa Gabor would wear. I glanced back at the closed door.

What the heck?

Well, he hadn't planned on sleeping in the same room, so maybe this is the kind of getup richy-rich ladies slumbered in.

I was a T-shirt, girl. I put my hand through the night slip, and it was nearly see-through. I cast it from me like it was plutonium.

I pulled out my *Save the Trees* T-shirt that I had worn under my uniform and smelled the pits, then slipped it on. It covered my ample butt, and that's all that mattered. I wiped off the makeup and inspected myself, looking like Broom Hilda with the white hair. Horrible. I looked 70, not 27.

I really wanted to talk to my dad. I couldn't wait to hear about his night. I wasn't exactly sure what I could tell him about mine.

I peeked out of the bathroom—or powder room. I guessed you called something that is all gold and mirrored a powder room.

Devlin was gone. I came out hesitantly and glanced around. Yep, gone. I breathed a sigh of relief and grabbed my phone. No reception. Darn. I jimmied up the window and stuck my cellphone outside to see if I could pick up a bar. Nothing.

I was drawn to the sounds of a horse pawing below me. I looked down to see Devlin atop a tremendous black steed. The bridle gleamed gold in the full moon's glow.

I caught my breath and pulled my phone back in the window. I hid behind the curtain and peeked out of the side.

He was petting the horse and leaned over to give it a piece of carrot. A light came on in the front porch, and Devlin spurred his horse into a gallop with a jab of his boots. He rose up on two legs before he flew away into the night. I took a deep breath.

In all truth, it was more like a sigh. What can I say? What girl isn't a sucker for a handsome stud on a stately steed? Lethal combo. I wish I had never put that image in my head.

Chapter 22

*W*hen I woke, Devlin was already talking business on the phone. He was speaking German. Hmmm, German. That's sexy. He had a severe but charming tone.

I darted out a quick glance from under my pillow. Devlin was sprawled out on the leather settee, conversing as if they were best friends. I could see why he could be successful.

Much better to deal with a good vibe than some stuffy bigwig. He had papers spread on the side table and the silver tray–*I bet real silver too—not that silver coating stuff that washes off*–with a pot of coffee and a small OJ.

He clicked off the call and got up to stoke the logs. He was already perfectly coifed and in a sleek gray suit that hugged his perfect physique.

"If you're done spying on me, you should dress for breakfast—we'll be leaving at 8:05. That gives you…" A glance at his watch— "ten minutes."

I opened full Betty Boop eyes from my lousy camouflaged spying spot under my pillow. Ten minutes? I reached up and felt my head. It would take me that long to get a brush through my new bush hair thanks to the murderous bleach. I prayed I could get it looking better than my current Phyllis Diller look.

****

We walked down the marble staircase. Devlin looked good enough to eat in his suit and sky-blue shirt. I was doing better with the shoes today, as they were only two inches high, instead of four.

Devlin had not only unpacked my new clothes for me, but also organized, hung up, and color-coded my part of the closet while I was sleeping.

For my breakfast introduction to the family, he had chosen a cream Chanel skirt and blazer combo *with sensible* nude shoes. Beneath the suit, I sported a silk blouse that made me feel like a real girl. Who knew polyester wasn't the blend of queens?

Huge busts of dead animals lined the walls cabin style, and I looked away, disgusted. Hunters were second on my list of evil. I looked up at Devlin, who eyed me critically. I was about to tell him how wrong it was to kill animals when he said, "Is that the best you could do with your hair?"

I scrunched up the side of my mouth and brought my hand to my hair. Unfortunately, the answer was *yes*.

"Well, it used to look good naturally, but now it's white straw, thanks a lot."

He pushed an errant strand behind my ears. "You don't have to hide your face. You look like a Muppet. Now stand up tall and look like I'd marry you."

I instinctively stuck out my tongue, but I did straighten my back. Jerk.

"Okay, lets practice," he said. "Ask me something about myself."

I rolled my eyes. A narcissist's favorite tune. "Okay, what is your favorite music?"

"Gershwin's Rhapsody in Blue."

"Mine is *Rogers & Hammerstein's Cinderella.*"

Devlin shook his head. "Cliché."

"What?" I said. "Every girl loves those songs. Horse, prince, true love? What's not to like?"

"That's what cliché means, Allie. Besides, I thought you were the one that said you were never going to fall into the trap of believing in love again…how all the men you love leave you, and all that?"

I made a prune face. I was not about to feel bad about loving some classic musical. I thought he had been sleeping when I was droning on about my failure with men, boosted by my sugar high from two glasses of chocolate milk. I didn't even want to think about it.

"Well, you should listen to the soundtrack. It's incredible. My mother and I used to sing along all the time. *Ten minutes ago, I met you; you looked up when I walked in the room.* So romantic."

"I've heard it."

He put a hand over my mouth. "I played the Prince at boarding school."

I laughed. "You sang too?"

He sneered. "It wasn't my choice. I needed an extra-curricular activity to get into Harvard. Moving on."

I suppressed a giggle. I liked the thought of big haughty Devlin having to dance around in tights and sing syrupy songs to the Cinderella musical. My kingdom for that videotape.

"Besides," Devlin said, looking down at me. "You don't believe in fairytale love, and neither do I. That's the one thing that does make us perfect together. You're just as much a commitment-phobe as I am."

I thought about that. Did hating men and swearing to be single my whole life mean I was a commitment-phobe? Better than brokenhearted and betrayed, in my book.

Devlin whined on. "Yep, completely un-marriable."

I cleared my throat and tried to change the subject.

"*Moving on.* What's your favorite drink?"

"Rothschild 68 Latour."

"Mine is chocolate milk."

"Favorite food?"

"Beef Wellington."

"Spam."

He shook his head again.

"I would never date you."

"Ditto," I spat back, as we entered the communal area. I arranged a pleasant smile on my face.

"I was kidding about the spam; I'm a vegetarian," I mumbled under my breath.

"Good, because I believe we're all out."

****

An older man let himself out of what looked to be a library, and Devlin stopped. "Hi, Dad," Devlin said tentatively. His dad turned slowly and looked confused.

Devlin walked over to him. "Dad, it's me. Devlin." He thrust out his hand as if it were a business meeting. The older man looked at his hand, then back at him.

"Devlin." The older Somerset hugged his son affectionately.

"I thought for a minute you didn't recognize me," said Devlin after the embrace. He sounded like a hurt little boy.

"No, of course not, son. I lost my darn glasses, and I'm just stubborn now about getting a new pair. When did you get in–just now?" He looked around, and his eyes caught mine.

"W-we got in late last night. I came to surprise you. You were probably half asleep; I should have called. "

He smiled. "So good to see you, lad. And who's this beauty?"

I gulped.

"My fiancé, Dad. "

The man studied me again. "Really? Well done, well done, both of you. Welcome to our home." He smiled all the way through to the heart. "Truly wonderful to have you both here. I couldn't be happier." His gray eyes crinkled with sincerity.

I felt the urge to come over and give him a little hug, because that's what I would have done if it were the real thing. I suddenly felt weird about the ruse. I hadn't really considered it all the way through, and how I'd have to be here lying to this kind old man grappling to hang on to his mind.

Inside I wanted to say, "Hey, Mr. Somerset. How are you? I miss our visits and you bringing me chocolate milk…" Instead, I was praying he didn't recognize me and implicate my father. I backed up quickly and hid behind Devlin.

Mr. Somerset ambled off toward the kitchen door. "Well, I'm off to help the young'uns build a proper snowman. There's perspective they need to consider. Not a mathematician between them. Enjoy breakfast." He nodded graciously.

"Oh, and Allie," he said lightly.

I went cold with fear that he was about to call me on my lie. Allie–we could have at least changed my darn first name.

I stiffened and said, "Yes, sir?"

"Watch out for the snakes." He laughed and waved as he went along on his mission.

I looked up at Devlin when I heard him catch his breath. It had been a long time since he'd seen his dad.

"You okay?" I mumbled as he watched his father struggle with his boots and finally get them on with the help of the butler.

He tried to walk out the door without his coat, but the sweet red-haired maid, Alice, stopped him and buttoned him up warm before allowing him out.

Devlin cleared his throat and pulled his eyes away. "I'm afraid Sissy's reports about Dad were right." He instinctively grabbed my hand and squeezed it. I tightened my fingers around his and looked up at him with empathy.

I had watched my mother deteriorate from cancer, her body slowing get weaker, but she had never lost her memory or mind. I couldn't imagine how that loss would feel.

His eyes met mine, and for a moment, we understood each other. Then he took a deep breath and pulled me into my first battle with the General.

Chapter 23

*W*e continued through the large glass doors to the

sunroom that was mainly a botanical garden filled with five
different colors of roses. Pink, yellow, red, orange, and
white. They grew everywhere in a floral rainbow
extravaganza. I inhaled the sweet smell and smiled at
Devlin.

  He frowned at me.

 "What?"

 "Favorite flower," I said. "Mine is rose."

  He stopped and looked around. The sunshine lit the
room and its bevy of glorious flowers.

  He smiled. "Ditto. Roses."

 "The perfect couple," I mocked.

He stopped and looked at me.
"Are you ready?"
I wasn't.
I nodded.
He grabbed my hand and squeezed it.
"Remember…"
"The weather is lovely, isn't it?" I said like a drone.

He smiled, and we continued on through the French
doors and out to the buffet breakfast that was being
served on the outdoor balcony.

Despite the cold, it was warm and cozy outside. There
were heaters along the edges of the stone balcony and a
fire at each end of the space. Jeeves and another man
that looked like a Chippendale dancer in full black and
whites stood at attendance at each end of a fancy buffet
of delicious delights.

The balcony had been decorated with lights and
mistletoe, and a solo violinist wove about the table and
played Christmas melodies like a music fairy.
I was stunned with the beauty of it all. So, this is how
billionaires did breakfast.

The balcony overlooked a spacious yard with marble
statues and an enclosed pool that looked like an
Olympian temple. Best yet, the Kissing Bridge ski
mountains in all their perfection were in full view.

Devlin held a chair for me, and I sat down with as
much grace as I could muster before coffee.

The table was long and elegant, and the only people seated were Sissy and her husband. I focused on the view. I consider myself able to get along with everyone—after two cups of coffee.

Coffee, please, before my fangs grow.

As if reading my mind, Jeeves appeared at my shoulder and leaned over and filled up my coffee cup. He offered me cream. I smiled in gratitude. I loved Jeeves. Jeeves good.

Devlin placed my napkin on my lap. I wrinkled my nose at him. "He loves to do that. Any excuse for him to touch me. Such a horny dog."

Devlin pinched me under the table.

Sissy looked up from her magazine and put her hand over her coffee cup as Jeeves approached. She dismissed him and waved over the handsome waiter, pointing to her empty champagne flute.

He hustled over to retrieve the bottle from the ice bucket and refill her glass. She watched his butt the entire time he poured her drink. I raised an eyebrow at Devlin, and he cleared his throat.

Kent, Sissy's husband, popped out from behind his newspaper cover. He wore a garish plaid suit and black Harry Potter glasses.

"Devlin. You showed up. Lovely to see you, old chap, it's been a while." He drawled in some weird English accent despite the fact Devlin had said he grew up in Santa Monica.

"Same, Kent. How's LA treating you?"

"Warmly. I'm not sure how I let Sissy talk me into this, instead of Hawaii."

Sissy dripped out. "No one knew you were coming for Christmas, Devlin. It's been a long time."

Devlin smiled back a matching icicle. "I don't remember you mentioning you were coming, either."

She motioned the hot guy to refill her flute again. I have to say, I didn't mind watching those glutes glide over at a closer range.

"Well, it's a surprise for both of us." Sissy scoffed and raised her glass.

I got busy focusing on my amazing-smelling croissant. On the table in front of me, there were three types of butter and two unidentified jellies to choose from. I looked at the condiment plate, hesitating. One spoon. Did I use the same spoon for all five sauces, or my own spoon? I put my hand down. Gosh, darn it! My kingdom for a good old Egg McMuffin with no bacon.

Devlin side-glanced over and nodded for me to follow his lead as he scooped the jelly onto his plate *with his own spoon*—and then his bread.

He winked at me, and something inside of me went to mush. He was much harder to hate when he wasn't making horrible faces at me.

"I know why you're here, Sissy. You might fool Dad, but you can't fool me."

"And I know *why you're here.*"

The standoff chill was palatable.

Sissy looked me up and down.

"The new one—*the porno Queen*—you brought home for Christmas, how very traditional of you."

I coughed.

"No, I'm not a porn star. That was…" I grasped for help from Devlin like a life preserver. "I'm in college…no strange dancing."

Devlin was glaring at his sister.

"Allie is my fiancé."

Her elegant brows rose in unison.

"Oh, that's rich."

My face flushed. Had she seen right through our ruse already? I swallowed and moved closer to Devlin to shield myself from her death stare. She seemed to have on some kind of contact lenses, so she looked like a deranged anime.

"Where's the ring?" she said, voice like syrup.

I stuck out my hand limply like it was a Gumby arm. The epic three-carat diamond sparkled and shone.

"Humph. A ring isn't a wedding. It won't work, Devlin. I know you. You're a playboy, and there is no way you are marrying anyone. You're not the marrying kind, but you know exactly what Dad wants."

I suddenly felt terrible for Devlin. She looked at him like he was dirt, too.

Sissy drank her champagne and stared at me over the disappearing bubbles. I focused on my plate. The waiter had just put down an elegant vegetarian omelet, and it looked way nicer than Scary Day Drunk Sissy.

"Sooooo…" she cooed dangerously. I glanced up, hoping she wasn't talking to me. She was.

I gulped.

"Exactly how did you meet my brother? You don't really look like his type."

My face flamed and I balled up my fist under the table. I judged her to be about 5'7" but super skinny. She probably threw up everything she ate when no one was looking. Skinny salad-eating Californian obviously didn't know she was messing with a Jersey girl. We had weight going for us.

Devlin reached over and undid my clenched fingers and brought my hand up to his mouth. He kissed my hand tenderly and stared into my eyes with fake affection.

"We bumped into each other outside of the Somerset building, actually. I took one look at her and knew she was the one. She had this funny cap on, and when it fell off– her blue eyes stopped my breath. Love at first sight."

He stared at me like he meant it.

"Y-yes I remember it well," I stuttered. "Swept me off my feet." Devlin looked me in the eye and then aimed a barb at his sister. "And I knew she was different from all the other spoiled rotten rich women I had known my whole life…"

He held up his coffee cup in mock salute.

Sissy brought up her hands and made a claw action back at Devlin.

"Pulling out the talons so early, Devlin, and you haven't even had a drink." She laughed a chortle that sounded like she needed to get her lungs checked.

"Nothing like a bunch of drunk Somersets to ruin a holiday, right Kent?"

Kent was back in his newspaper, and I wish he could have offered me even part of it. I'm pretty sure he wasn't even looking at the cartoon section.

Devlin squeezed my hand and returned it to me. I looked at it like it was a foreign invader, then stuck it on my lap and played with my napkin.

"Balderdash! I don't drink during the day, Sissy," Devlin spat back. "We've got big things going on with Somerset Industries. I've been on the phone trying to keep one of our biggest accounts all morning. We need to make changes to compete! I'm hoping you'll get on my side and help Dad see that he needs to let me take over now so I can save our family business."

She laughed. "Good luck."

Devlin stiffened beside me.

Jeeves pushed the waiter toward refilling Sissy's glass, and she luckily went back to looking inappropriately at his butt.

Chapter 24

*N*ow, I really did mean to keep my mouth shut. I

certainly wasn't going to bring up the rainforest or the fact that Somerset Industries killed more trees for stupid boxes than anyone, and that directly impacted global warming.

No. I was going to be the perfect, quiet well-heeled fiancé. But since I am neither well-heeled nor a fiancé, it was only a matter of time before I would mess up even with the best intentions.

Breakfast with the Somersets was about as much fun as Russian roulette. Between the evil sneers, rotten barbed comments, and just plain condescendence, it was hard to get my good eat on, despite the lavish spread.

I love breakfast, and I'm not above ordering the *Hungry Man Breakfast* with the all-you-can-eat pancakes.

I don't have a weight problem, so I guess it's okay that I can eat my own weight in veggie sausage. But it can get a little embarrassing when everyone else is just drinking coffee and trading insults.

I, for one, think they would have enjoyed themselves a lot more if they kept their mouths occupied with some good old feasting.

After all, it was Christmas. I watched below as the children played with Mr. Somerset and attempted to place the big snowball pieces on top of each other

"He looks like a great grandpa," I offered. I had never gotten to know mine.

Sissy snorted and splashed her drink around drunkenly. "I wish he could have put that act on for us when we were kids." She sounded so bitter, and I wondered if I misjudged how perfect things were from my outside view.

"Well, he looks like he's trying now…" her husband said, without looking up from his newspaper.

"He's a good actor." Sissy fingered her champagne flute.

My gut dropped at the venomous comment. I straightened and tried to offer something to the conversation.

"Devlin mentioned some memory issues–is there anything we can do?" I asked, concerned as I took a miniature bite of my omelet.

Sissy glared at me.

"That would be none of your business. Some part-time girlfriend of my brother's has no concern for what goes on in the inner circle of the Somerset dynasty."

I felt the slap without the physical touch. My face reddened. Was caring about someone considered low class now? Who knew, with these people? I usually had a quick sarcastic comeback for random insults like this, but throwing Sissy Somerset to the ground in front of the buffet table did not work in my Eliza Doolittle plan today.

For a moment, I felt just like I had when I was a child. Not good enough. Outsider. Keep your mouth shut; no one cares what the help's daughter has to say.

Suddenly her bloodshot eyes zeroed in on me, and she pointed. "You. How do I know that face, those googly blue eyes…?"

Of course, that just made my eyes Betty Boop even more. I wanted to lean in and say, *That's right sister, I'm back like Chucky's revenge.* "Remember the art studio?" I wanted to ring out like my own personal Alamo.

Suddenly, I felt firm hands on my shoulders, steadying me. I hadn't realized I'd been shaking until Devlin stopped me. I looked up at his face, thankful, and was thrown off guard by the look of defense he had on his.

"That's no way to talk to my fiancé. Of course, it matters. I agree that I…" He looked down at me with a flash of guilt. "I haven't visited in a long time, and I had no idea Dad had deteriorated."

Sissy threw back her champagne. "He hides it from you. Doesn't want you thinking you can steal his job."

Devlin's face went deep scarlet and his eyes nearly closed.

"I'm trying to help the family business. I'm not trying to steal anything. You don't know what's going on; you're not there every day. I am."

"You have always been a better playboy than businessman, Devlin. Convince him to sell with me and get back to doing what you do best." She tossed her hand in my direction like she was trying to shoo away a fly.

Her perfect blonde hair was in the perfect place. Her forty-year-old skin pulled back just enough to look like a thirty-year-old with functional plastic surgery.
I touched my hair that matched her shade and realized I hated blonde hair more than ever.

"Sell?!"

Devlin thrust himself from his seat, sending the table shaking.

"Who said anything about selling?"

Sissy looked like an archer that had hit her mark. A slow, self-satisfied smirk crossed her face.

"You think you're the only one that has a stake in this business, Devlin? Just because I'm not there in New York, privy to the day to day minutiae doesn't mean it's not my concern."

Devlin's eyes grew stormy, and the tornado was aimed right at his sister. I pulled back to avoid being sucked into the caustic spiral.

"And just what *is* your concern, Sissy?"

"From what I see, we're going to be dinosaurs soon. I saw the news–it does make it out to California, you know."

Devlin whistled out an annoyed hoot. "You mean between yoga classes and kale smoothies, you catch the Kardashians talking about it? I live and breathe our business every day. We need to make some big decisions, but Somerset Industry is not for sale. That's FINAL."

She laughed, bitter sounding and brittle. "We'll see about that."

Chapter 25

I excused myself from the table to go hang out with the

kids and Mr. Somerset, and to make a snowman. It had to be way more fun than playing in this minefield with these Somersets.

I switched into some suitable snow-romping clothes and joined the group in the yard.

I really had a good time with the children, and enjoyed pelting them with snowballs since they were new to this environment. I could easily win. They laughed and threw the soft snowballs with glee, but they didn't know about mixing them with a little ice to make them really hurt. I wasn't about to share that.

After we finished our snow fight, we got down to serious business and assembled a *beautiful and symmetrical snowman*. Mr. Somerset was directing the construction of the snowman parts in a very serious manner.

The children had never seen snow, so they were over the moon playing in the winter wonderland.

I even taught them how to do snow angels, and before long, we had fifty angels between the five of us. Even Mr. Somerset got in a good snow angel before Jeeves urged him off the ground and back to directing from the chair they had brought down for him.

About an hour later, Alice came to retrieve us from our snow play, announcing it was time for the Christmas cookie baking lessons.

Only rich people.

Chapter 26

*T*he kitchen hummed with activity. Pierre, the chef, had arranged for his dear friends, the Landers sisters, to visit and show us the proper way to make a Christmas cutout cookie.

Pierre was in awe of the sisters. He fluttered around them, flapping his hands and murmuring French I couldn't understand. "Ooh la la, Ladies Landers. I can cook, but I cannot bake; you are superb!" He motioned to Carol and Ethel, who smiled over the compliments. "Blue ribbon winners for the last 70 years. They're famous in Kissing Bridge!"

The sisters blushed, and I thought how adorable they looked in their matching gray dresses and pristine white aprons. They looked like they had leaped out of a Julia Child book ready to be of service. They both hugged me affectionately, and I blushed at their kindness.

Sissy was absent, thankfully, but all five of her children, including the baby with his nanny, were in attendance. The kids were thrilled to be in a cookie-making class and enthusiastically tied on little aprons that made them look sweet and much less entitled.

Little Kent junior beamed up at me.

"Super fun, right?!"

I smiled back. "Yeah, super fun."

He stuck both his hands in his flour mixture and tossed a big gust in the air. It came down like a shower and dusted both of us nearly pure white.

I wiped the flour out of my eyes and Kent beamed. "And nobody cares if we—"

I reached out my hand and touched his shoulder.

"Yes, people care if you have manners, Kent." He raised a young, aristocratic brow.

I pointed to the various staff, and the Landers bent over, helping the other children.

"These people want you to have fun, but if you make an extra mess, it won't be so fun for them."

I gestured toward the maid, Alice. " They will have to spend extra time cleaning up your mess."

He looked at me and nodded.

"But after this, we can have a re-game on that snowball fight, and you can try and pepper me as hard as you want. Deal?"

He laughed. "Deal."

Devlin came into the kitchen dressed in an all-black designer suit and looking like a billion dollars. His eyes met mine.

He stared at the flour all over my face and shook his head.

Jeeves came forward. "Can I get you anything, sir, or would you care to join your father and sister in the library?"

"My sister?"

The butler raised one eyebrow and nodded. "Yes, sir."

Devlin looked at me, and then strode away toward the library. He disappeared down the hall and, when the door opened, I could hear arguing coming from the inside.

I dusted myself off and asked the Landers sisters for *official permission to bake.*

Carol Landers came over to inspect my cookies. I had chosen the Christmas tree cutout, and now the tree cookies were lined up on the baking sheet like a mini forest.

She clapped me on the back and some flour puffed out of my hair. Kent clapped his hand over his mouth to stifle a laugh. I stuck my tongue out at him.

"Perfect, Allie. Just the right amount of golden butter color, and all your cutouts are very proportioned." She nodded approval.

I smiled.

"Permission to bake?" I said like a soldier.

"Approved." She smiled back. "Upper oven, middle rack for 11 minutes."

I saluted and moved off with my glorious cookies to the oven.

I set a timer for 11 minutes and decided to go outside in the yard to see if I could catch reception and call my dad. I had filled him in on the time frame, but that was about it.

I slipped out of the kitchen and went to find my parka. Jeeves had put it in one of the closets–but which of the darn ten closets was that?

I tiptoed past the library, and the door was ajar.

Devlin was upset.

"I don't think you understand. China Box is undercutting us on one side, and Bamazon has switched to plastic, so that account has been cut in half."

I gasped. The only thing worse than boxes made from trees was plastic. That was totally horrible for the planet!

I had spent days on the Jersey coast on Earth Day weekend, picking up plastic refuse. It never goes away. This was terrible news. I glanced around to see if any of the servants were hovering, but it was only me. I leaned in closer.

Sissy was equally incensed by the conversation. "That's exactly why we should sell NOW. Before our company is worthless. Besides, Dad isn't capable of dealing with all this stress. "

Devlin whistled through his teeth. "Dad hasn't been dealing with it–I have! As I've been dealing with all the hundreds of thousands of people we employ around the country, Sissy. Great Grandfather would never sell out his employees who made him successful."

I cocked my head. I had never heard Devlin say anything remotely caring about anyone other than himself. Now here he was, going to bat against Satan on behalf of the little man?

Sissy slammed something, and I heard broken glass, then Jeeves rushing to clean it up. I pulled back.

Mr. Somerset intervened in a slow, unsteady whisper. "The employees do matter. I agree with Devlin."

Devlin hissed out a relieved sound. "Thank you, Father, for believing in me."

"But…" said the older Somerset. "The China Box takeover and Bamazon changes are a huge impact. We can't be caught with our britches down…"

Devlin sputtered. "I have a plan–I just need to get some numbers to explain the whole vision…."

"Good. We'll talk tomorrow, then you show me why I shouldn't agree with your sister."

Devlin suddenly burst through the door, brows knit together, and strode toward the kitchen.

I slunk back and breathed a sigh when I spotted my parka. Thank goodness it was in only the third darn closet I checked. No wonder they needed Jeeves to help them find anything.

I put on the parka and moved toward the side back door when I heard Sissy speaking. I looked around and hovered closer to the door, acting as if I were admiring the Picasso in the hall.

I opened my mouth in disgust as she rattled off lie after lie about Devlin being irresponsible and flighty. It was so untrue. I barely knew him, but there was no denying how much he put into the business.

"Here, Dad, just sign this paper, and it will be done. The company is sold. No more headaches. You deserve it, Daddy," she said in a corn fructose sugar way.

"You want me to sign this? Maybe I should read it first, don't you think, or have my lawyer…"
"I had a lawyer in California draft it up. Trust me. I know China Box will offer us a price you can't say no to."

China Box? Both my eyebrows went up at once. I knew all about the vast foreign company that had already swallowed up thousands of jobs around the country.

Even in Jersey, plants had closed, and jobs had been lost and outsourced because of China Box's growth. Somerset Industries had had to cut over a thousand jobs in a downsizing attempt to compete, and that was just in our state.

I suddenly felt an odd kinship with Devlin, despite my disgust for him. I held my breath and prayed that Mr. Somerset wasn't going to sign whatever Sissy was pushing at him.

****

I saw Devlin stride through the back kitchen door, and I ran after him.

Outside it was still a cold, clear day, and the wind whipped my hair like little stingers, but I kept running and within a moment I was by his side and breathless. He looked at me oddly and back to where I had come from, confused by my sudden appearance.

I huffed and puffed. "What are you doing out here?" he asked as he continued toward the stables.

I followed him.

"Look, Devlin. We have to really double down on this. There's so much at stake."

"Tell me something I don't know," he said without breaking stride.

I struggled to keep up with him. "Look, we both are on the same team."

He cocked his head." Since when?"

"Since I happened to overhear some of your conversation in the library," I said sheepishly.

He shook his head and trudged forward.

"I think you can come up with a solution. Economize and keep your account with Bamazon."

"Glad you are so optimistic. From what I see, I'm about to put hundreds of thousands of employees out of work if I don't figure this out."

I grabbed his hand to stop him because I couldn't keep up.

"Listen. I want to help you. I care about people's jobs as much as I care about the environment. Plastic isn't the solution either. I already started a petition against Bamazon to stop that. It's cheaper, but it's as bad as killing trees. It kills the ocean."

Devlin's mouth went firm and straight, and he dead-eyed me.

"You really did listen?"

I shrugged.

"So, what's your solution then?"

I swallowed. Solution? That was the problem. I always saw the problem, but rarely found the answer. That was the sad part. You want to help, but in the end, you can only gripe about it, and then nothing happens.

"I'm not sure, but there are natural alternatives you might look into that are cheaper. I mean, in the end, all the companies are going to have to revolutionize sooner or later– why not Somerset Industries be the first?"

Devlin glanced at me with what resembled respect. I'm sure I was wrong.

But he did say, "I'm not against it. I don't need to wait until the fourth quarter and see my competition has changed and I'm out of two hundred fifty million dollars' profit. Being on the forefront is key in business at our level."

"Exactly. I can't recommend anything now, but let me think about it."

"Think quickly." He opened the barn door.

We entered the large wooden barn that housed the stables. I looked down the long lanes with elegant horses peeking out of their stalls to see who had come to visit.

"Oh, what pretty stables." I looked around at the rustic, western-decorated walls. It too had the standard royal chandelier and a roaring fire. The homey smell of hay and the whinnies of the horses made it feel comforting

A stableman dressed in a plaid shirt and jeans, who Devlin addressed as Roy, came out of the side office and tipped his cowboy hat.

"Wondering when I'd see you, Mr. Devlin." He grinned broadly, and he was missing one tooth.

Devlin smiled. "I actually slipped in late last night to give Majestic a run."

The stableman nodded in my direction. "Howdy, miss"

"Oh, Roy, may I introduce my fiancé?"

Roy beamed. "Nice to meet you, truly, miss"

"You too, Roy. I love horses." I smiled. "Can I pet them?"

Devlin nodded. "Hold on." He reached in his pocket. "You want to make a friend, feed them some of these."

He handed me some cut apple pieces, and I wandered over to a pretty white mare that looked friendly.

I could hear Devlin chatting amiably with the stable guy and felt relieved for a moment. The stable felt safe, and I relaxed for the first time all night.

"Hey, beauty," I said as I held out an apple for the pretty white horse. She was on the small side, and she nibbled the treat out of my hand gently. I felt emboldened, and I reached up and stroked her nose.

"So…" Devlin joined me. "I see you've met our lovely Daisy." He rubbed her nose, and she nuzzled him back. "Hey, girl, how are you?"

"She's a sweetheart."

"She sure is."

I petted her again and felt the soft fur of her nose. "How about if I give you your first riding lesson?" Devlin said.

I looked around the barn and the horses and took a deep breath. I had never ridden a horse, let alone some spirited purebred owned by the Somersets. I looked up at Devlin for reassurance, and he squeezed my hand.

"I'll teach you. You'll love it."

I swallowed.

"And you can't go wrong with our little Daisy."

I nodded. Of course, Devlin Somerset's fiancée would be expected to know how to ride. He was like some Duke that had fallen out of an Outlander movie with his servants and stables.

He grabbed my hand and led me toward the saddles and tack. "I have a saddle that my grandma wouldn't fall out of."

I followed him. He had changed into jeans, and they hugged him in just the right way. I bit my lip. I was scared to death, but it had nothing to do with the horses.

Chapter 27

*D*evlin lifted me up and sat me on the gentle, white mare.

"Daisy is a sweetheart. You have nothing to worry about. We start the toddlers on her."

I nodded. Toddlers. Good. Perfect.

"You okay?" he asked.

I smiled. No, I was scared as all heck, but I wouldn't tell him that.

He gave me a brief explanation of the reins and how to get Daisy to stop. Devlin looked at me and smiled.

"You've never been on a horse before, have you?"

"Merry go round."

He laughed. "Figures. Just follow me, I'll help you."

After a brief lesson, we ambled down a pine-forested path. I breathed in the fresh mountain air.

"These trees are amazing," I said, appreciating the tall pines.

Devlin looked at them. "I guess they are. We grow acres of trees for our boxes."

"Yes, but they never get this old before you chop them down. These have to be at least a couple hundred years old. Do you know some of the trees in the Amazon rainforest are over three thousand years old?"

"Really." He frowned. "No, I didn't."

"Irreplaceable. And acres being burned for burgers and palm oil."

I was starting to build up my usual ire over the greed that was eating up what should be a world treasure.

He glanced down at me riding next to him. His horse was a good six hands higher than mine, and it reared and snorted like it wanted to race. Devlin reined in its enthusiasm, expertly handling the spirited animal.

"You're really good with horses."

He looked at me. "They're good for me. I spent most of my time at the stables after..." He looked away into the distance.

"How many times I ran these trails hoping to outrun my own thoughts." He looked at me, and my eyes met his in understanding.

Between my mother passing away and my ex's betrayal, I had shriveled away from life. The world had been tainted, and I had just needed to get as far away as possible. I had become a hermit myself for years with nothing but my activism to inspire me.

I focused on the path ahead and tried to keep my own horrid memories at bay. The rhythmic rocking of the horse's gait and the steady clip-clop on the snow was calming. A squirrel scampered across the path, chased by his buddy leaving tiny print marks on the snow.

"I see why you could fall in love with horseback riding," I said as Devlin brought his horse next to mine once more.

It was hard to look at him sitting on the horse and keep hating him. Between the hot guy pose on a stallion and his vulnerability leaking out I was going to have double down on why I hated Devlin Somerset.

When I dared a glance, he was staring at me.

"I found out that you can't outrun yourself no matter how fast you gallop."

"How exactly fast do you need to go for that to happen?" I joked.

He laughed and grabbed my reins to steady our horses next to each other.

"So, I'm not the only one with problems."

I snorted unattractively, and then covered my nose.

"Ahh, no. My life is pretty much on code red right now. I don't know what I would have done if our deal hadn't come along. We, well, we need it for our house. Mom's medical bills mounted up."

Devlin looked at me for the first time like he really saw me as a person." Ahhh. So, you just didn't fancy to buy some sports car with the money?"

I blushed. Like I'd ever buy a car that wasn't electric, please. "No. No Ferrari."

He nodded. "I've been kind of sheltered. I've seen the world, but I haven't seen much of your part."

I struggled to keep hating him. He was making it really hard with his authentic personality sneaking out.

"You're lucky. You'll never have to worry about someone dying and you not being able to have enough money to do anything about it." I chewed my lip. I didn't need to share my personal issues with my fake billionaire fiancé. He would never understand, anyway.

I glanced over at him looking like a Greek God on his horse and saw his pensive look. I suddenly remembered hearing from my father that Devlin's mother had died when he was young. Here I was complaining about life and fate.

I gurgled out an awkward apology. "I'm sorry. I heard your mother died of a stroke. That must have been horrible."

He shook his head. "Yes, and very sudden."

I swallowed hard; my heart ached for him.

"I'd gotten in trouble, and we had a fight. So, I decided to run away," he confessed. "I made it all the way to

Jeeves' back house where I hid out, trying to teach her a lesson. My mother thought I was lacking in my pursuit of becoming a perfect gentleman, and she was right, of course." He laughed a sad, choked sound. "She died that night."

My face melted in sympathy.

He glanced at me, and his eyes were a tornado of thoughts. "I blamed myself."

"But a stroke can't be caused by an argument Devlin."

He shook his head. "I know. The doctor sat us all down and told us how strokes work. Still, I blamed myself. I guess we all have regrets."

He looked like that lost five-year-old boy again.

I reached out and touched his arm. It felt raging hot, and his muscles tensed when I touched him.

"I'm so sorry."

He shook his head.

"A long time ago."

We continued down the snowy path, and I pet Daisy's soft neck.

"So, your father, he never remarried?"

Devlin shook his head. "No. Well, not officially. After that, we lost him to work. He buried himself and his sadness. I was raised by a continued rotation of nannies because we were *difficult* or, should I rephrase that, because Sissy was evil."

I laughed. Sissy *was* evil! Almost at a comical level–like full-on Disney villain bad.

"That must've been hard."

He shrugged. "Nobody feels sorry for a rich kid."

My face flushed.

I was one of those people. I often wondered how people couldn't see the person behind the circumstance—as if being homeless made you subhuman—but now I realized that maybe I hadn't been seeing rich people as human either. I suddenly had a new understanding of Devlin and perhaps the wrong way I'd been looking at the world.

Chapter 28

*D*evlin motioned for me to follow him. "Come see this. I want to show you something."

   We walked our horses through a canopy of snow-dappled trees into a clearing with a stunning enclosed gazebo. It was a grand building made of white marble with golden scrolls in the shape of Cinderella's carriage. The windows were lit from inside with crystal chandeliers.

   Devlin slid off his horse like a prince and lifted his arms up to help me off. I tried not to notice how his hands felt on my hips. He motioned me over to look through the windows. "This is where we will have the Mistletoe Ball on Christmas Eve."

"Like the balls you used to have in Long Island?"

He nodded. "Yes. This is our Chalet Ballroom. Dad had it built, especially to host this event."

It was stunning, and I was freaked out. He had mentioned that we had special affairs we were to attend, but this was the Somersets' Ball! I had dreamed of visiting the magical event when I was a child. The beautiful dresses and elegantly-dressed men waltzing like spinning teacups. But the reality was that the grown-up me had no idea how to fancy dance! My heart sank.

"I don't suppose they'll be fast dancing? Hokey pokey or anything I might actually know how to do?"

Devlin arched one brow. "No. No hokey pokey."

I sighed. "Too bad. I'm excellent at the hokey pokey."

He smiled at me, and I blushed like an idiot.

"My parents met at a Christmas dance and got caught under the mistletoe, and that began their lifelong love. My father still insists on having a ball every year in my mother's honor."

It reminded me of my mom and her charity event I didn't make. My heart hurt at missing it, but I hoped Dad was spreading the joy and would bring back pictures to show me.

I looked through the window at the inside of the magnificent ballroom. "How romantic. They must have been very much in love."

"Yes, very much."
I grabbed his hand instinctively and squeezed it.

Chapter 29

I had so much to think about, and I was filled with dread.

I had never been to a super formal dance. Sissy was already suspicious of Devlin. Any more faux pas on my part, and I might blow it for both of us.

I had also learned more about who Devlin really was.

"Your first real ride. Well done," he said sincerely.

I beamed. As much from the praise as from the closeness. His strong hands lifted me in one motion to the ground. Our eyes locked. I slipped into his embrace, and he pulled me close against his muscular chest. My knees felt weak, and I wiggled away from his touch. This was a business deal, and I needed to stay on my toes.

"Thank you. That was really great. I loved it."

Suddenly, my hands flew to my mouth.

"Oh, my cookies!"

Devlin laughed. "That's a new one."

"No, I mean oh my goodness, I've burned my cookies I had in the oven. I forgot all about them!" I started to run from the stables, but he caught me around the waist with one arm.

Devlin smiled. "I'm sure Pierre has it covered by now." He pulled me closer into his arms, and I stopped breathing.

"You have more important things to consider than cookies right now," he said teasingly.

"I do?"

He nodded bemusedly.

"What next, bungee jumping? Paragliding over the mountains?"

He chuckled. "Not quite that dangerous."

He slipped off his coat, then came around and helped me remove mine. He put them on a hook and adjusted the lighting lower. Finally, he flipped a switch and music came on.

I looked up at the lofts of the stables. It glowed with warmth and was lit by an out-of-place, glorious chandelier that hung amid the wooden beams and lofts of hay. Chandeliers seemed to be the standard in every room the Somersets owned.

Suddenly, I was in Devlin's arms. My heart beat fast, and breath escaped my lips. No fake kissing, I hoped.

"I believe this is the best and safest place to begin your waltzing lessons."

I laughed. "Right."

He dead-eyed me. "I can only imagine that if you've never learned to properly ride a horse, your cultural influence may have stopped at learning to waltz for a ball."

"You would have imagined correctly." I smiled.

"Now follow me. We're going to move in the shape of a box. Just lean in and I'll guide you. Step, step, step–look up at me, not at your feet."

I did.

"Good." He pulled me in close and spun me around, and I laughed.

"Loosen up. Dancing can be fun–and sexy." He pulled me near, and I had an ultra closeup of his cleft chin. The scar from the diamond wound had healed perfectly. I tensed when I felt his muscles press against me, but I fell into his movements swirling us together.

"Just press your body into mine, feel me…"

Goodness, how much could one girl handle? I sucked in my breath and closed my eyes and tried to feel him as he moved. Step, step, step. One two three, one two three...

The lovely waltz played on, and we danced and danced.

I am not a quick study, but I am strong-minded. I lost myself in the moment, dancing with full dedication. I forgot time and found the present and finally understood what all those darn yoga classes were trying to get me to feel.

The bevy of horses whinnied from their stalls in harmony to the lilting music, and I felt like I might never come back to Earth again. I closed my eyes and tried to implant this memory on my mind forever, and suddenly I felt firm, wanting lips on mine.

Devlin pressed me in closer to his tight body, and I felt like an arcade machine that had just lit up all over. I didn't even try to stop him. I'm going to admit it: I'd never been kissed like that by a real boyfriend, let alone some fake stand-in. I fell headlong into a spiral of soft lips and strong hands.

When he pulled away, I nearly fell over. That would have been classy. I straightened up and cleared my throat.

Devlin was beaming at me now. "Nobody would ever guess we were faking being in love."

I shot him the thumbs up like a doltz, and then decided to exit stage left as quickly as possible. I had to get myself out of there before I did anything stupid. Like, kiss that hunk again, *fakely of course.*

I walked out of the stables with my dignity, and my head held high. But as soon as I cleared Devlin's sight, I found myself running down the path back to the house at a speed that would have made my track coach proud. I never even saw Sissy by the door of the stable...nodding with satisfaction.

Chapter 30

T hat night, I was looking forward to some solo time –or,
more clearly, time away from Devlin and Ursula from
California.

   The whole troop was headed off to enjoy the epic
mountain up at Eagle's Peak. The Somersets were all
expert skiers, so I feigned a headache.

   I couldn't bear to fail at another passion that these
people seemed born with. Rushing down a massive
mountain on a little board? For fun? No, I wasn't about to
risk my life to *fit in* with people I'd *never* fit in with. Skiing
trips to Vail and Aspen had never been in our family
budget.

Instead, I invented an enjoyable alternative to get myself out of the family ski adventure without making anyone suspicious.

I had asked Pierre if he would be so kind as to teach me how to make Devlin's favorite dish, *Beef Wellington*.

Goodness, even the children needed to lighten up. I was glad to see them so excited about going skiing. Young Kent ran by us in the kitchen, ready to run out without his boots.

"Ahh, Kent," I said.

He skidded to a stop and waved at us. "Hi, Chef! Hi, Allie! I'm going snowboarding—Dad gave me a Christmas gift early, and I can't wait to try it out!" He held up his neon-colored snowboard.

I beamed at his excitement. "You just might want to put on some boots before you conquer the mountain."

He looked down at his feet. "Yeah, right. Jeeves!" He called for the butler.

Jeeves came running with the boots, as if he were physic. He winked at me as he helped the young man on with them. "I spotted the crisis from the dining hall, Ms. Allie."

Kent Sr. was all revved up and dressed in his ski suit—also plaid. Good grief, Sissy's ugly contacts must be making her hard of sight.

"Allie, you're not going?"

I shook my head.

"I'm afraid I'd hold you guys back. You're all pros and… I'm safer here." I mumbled the last part to myself. I could see myself losing control like a spaz and ending up in some icy pond or something. No, the kitchen was safe. Good things happened there, and bad things were made better doused in butter and sugar.

The Somersets all filed out into a large van that Kent Sr. had rented. Devlin appeared at my side and placed a perfunctory kiss on my cheek. I blushed and brought my hand to my cheek.

"I'll see you later, honey."

I recovered my coolness and raised a hand in goodbye. "Have a great time. I'm making a surprise for you."

Devlin looked back and forth between us, then nodded. "Great. Come on, Dad, let me help you with your coat."

"I don't need help." Mr. Somerset grumbled. Jeeves hovered near, and Devlin shook his head.

"Okay, Dad, but don't think I'm giving you any breaks on the slopes. I'm hoping you're old enough for me to beat you finally."

His dad laughed and clapped his hand on his son's back.

*****

I had a wonderful evening with the staff and Pierre. Since the whole family was gone, many of the servants had gathered in the kitchen around the sizable comfy fireplace to chat and eat as they had some time to themselves. There was a large oak table in front of it, and it was the perfect gathering place. I suppose Devlin and his type preferred the fancy, uncomfortable formal dining area, but I much preferred being in the kitchen.

Making Beef Wellington was a complicated, advanced-level dish. It involved all sorts of layers and strange ingredients and then a delicate sauce that was hard to master. Pierre had been happy to do it, and I was delighted to be hanging with the servants who were much more relaxed than the stuffy Somerset family.

Pierre instructed me patiently for what seemed hours, but together we prepared a feast for the staff and a tray of Beef Wellingtons for the Somerset family when they returned from skiing.

In any case, I had to save one for Devlin. He had told me it was his favorite, and I hoped he liked it. No, I wasn't a three-star Michelin chef, but I had just been schooled by one.

Chapter 31

*D*evlin was in the living room doing business when I came in the next morning. He had left me a handwritten note thanking me for the Beef Wellington, and I was excited to hear more. I don't know why the thought of pleasing Devlin me happy.

When I entered the grand living room, Devlin was on the settee in front of the fire, speaking French to someone. I don't know French, but it seemed as if he were trying to talk them into something. Or maybe French just always sounds like it's seducing you into something. Either way, I felt a flush of heat rise up my body. French does that to me.

Sissy breezed into the room and brought a chill with her. The nanny followed in her wake, holding the baby at her side. I tried not to catch Sissy's gaze. Her crazy anime contact lenses made her eyes extra scary to encounter first thing in the morning.

Mr. Somerset waved Sissy over. "Come join me, Sissy, you used to love puzzles, and I think this old head could use some help." He smiled hopefully.

"Dad, I love you, but I hate puzzles and watching you pick up and drop things like something out of *Rain Man* is not what I call fun."

I gasped. She smiled and whispered, "Don't worry; he doesn't remember a thing. The beautiful thing about Alzheimer's is you can finally tell your horrible parents what you actually think of them." She made the loco sign, and then looked at Jeeves and snapped at him, pointing to her shoulder, which was her sign to *get my darn coat.*

I glanced at Mr. Somerset involved in his Christmas puzzle, and he seemed blissfully unaware of his daughter's hatred for him.

"I'm going shopping—care to go?" Sissy said to me as she looked me up and down. Luckily, I was wearing a tailored cream suit—some kind of designer outfit that seemed to meet her approval because she didn't say anything nasty. "Devlin gave you his credit card at least?"

I looked over at Mr. Somerset by himself, trying to figure out where to put a piece of the puzzle. He looked at the piece and put it down, defeated. My heart went out to him.

"No, I'll just hang out here. I like puzzles." I lied.
I hated puzzles because I'm hyperactive and puzzle-doing requires focus and sitting for a long time. Still, I felt sorry for Mr. Somerset. Whatever reason Sissy despised him, he was still her father.

Jeeves returned with a red fox fur coat. I'm sure it was real, and I wished someone from PETA would have jumped out from behind the chaise lounge and doused her with pig's blood.

He helped her on with it, and Sissy leaned over and fake kissed her baby before strolling out of the living room. I heard her screaming for her husband to get the car.

I shook my head and tried to shake out Sissy's toxic vibe. I moved over and watched Mr. Somerset with Jeeves by his side doing the Christmas puzzle. The puzzle was of a beautiful Rockwell scene. I pointed to a red piece that fit in the mistletoe hanging part.

Mr. Somerset smiled at me and moved the piece into its proper place.

He motioned for me to sit down. "Join me, Allie."
I shrugged, plopped down, and considered the puzzle. It was half done, but it was intricate.

"Can I get something for you, Ms. Allie?" Jeeves bowed to me. I loved Jeeves. I opened my mouth, and Mr. Somerset said,

"Chocolate milk, isn't it?"

I stiffened and nodded.

Did he remember me, or had he seen me drink chocolate milk recently? I looked at Mr. Somerset, who found another piece and set it into the puzzle with a satisfactory nod.

The puzzle was filling in, and it was no help from me, I can tell you. I did a whole lot of watching. Devlin was pacing and passionate on the phone, and Mr. Somerset was slamming out this Rubik's cube of a puzzle.

I pondered this as I watched him expertly place another piece into the puzzle. It made me wonder just how much Mr. Somerset remembered or didn't.

"You're pretty good at this," I said with admiration.

He looked up swiftly.

"I'm just good with numbers and deduction."

"I bet that helped you build Somerset Industries into the great success it is today."

He nodded. "Yes. Partly. I gave up a lot—too much." His eyes met mine, and he looked anything but losing his mind.

"You're not really losing your memory, are you?" I suddenly spat out what I was thinking.

He smiled slowly, and a gleam came to his eyes. "Ahh, yes. You bought my darling daughter's story that I was losing my mind, huh? Alzheimer's, isn't it, Jeeves?" He laughed and made the loco sign near his head.

I smiled. "So, you're not losing your mind!"

Mr. Somerset snickered mischievously.

"She wishes."

I let out my breath and glanced over at Devlin, who was now engaged in a new conversation with equal fervor. He was speaking– Czech? How many languages did he speak fluently? I was starting to get impressed in spite of myself.

I looked back at his father. "Well, that's great news, Mr. Somerset. I don't know how people got the wrong idea."

He put a piece in the puzzle and said, "I'm the one that gave them the idea."

My mouth fell open in that oh-so attractive way.

Mr. Somerset laughed.

"Don't think too bad of me, dear. You see, I've always found the best way to see the pure soul of a person is how they treat you when they think you're down."

I looked at him. "You mean like Jesus in the Bible?"

Mr. Somerset hesitated with his puzzle piece and fixed his eyes on me.

"That's one example. He dressed as a homeless person to see the true being. Confucius had a saying along the lines of *when an elephant is down, even a frog will kick him.*'"

He placed the last piece in the puzzle with finality and gave me a wink. "Sadly, my dear. I think my children are both frogs."

I looked over his shoulder, but Devlin was still immersed in his business call. I leaned over the puzzle and looked him in the eye. I wondered if he knew who I was? I hated lying to him, but I had made a deal with Devlin.

"Listen to me, Mr. Somerset. No matter what happens, okay, I want you to know this."

He stopped and looked at me.

"Your son …I know Devlin would do anything—truly, go to any lengths—to be the man you want him to be, Mr. Somerset." I glanced at Devlin across the room, and his gray eyes met mine.

"But he is just a man, Mr. Somerset. Human like all of us. Just don't judge him too harshly. Promise me."

The older man studied me.

"You care about him," he said. "I can see that much."

I swallowed.

"He's not a frog, Mr. Somerset."

Chapter 32

$\mathcal{T}$he Christmas Fair at the Kissing Bridge Main Center

was the place to be. All the residents were out selling or buying gifts for the holidays. A group of carolers sang lovely songs around the town tree that was decorated with ornaments the children of the town had made. It was enchanting.

Even Devlin seemed at ease in the holiday joy. He chatted amiably with neighbors that passed, and when he slipped his arm through mine, it felt right. It was too good a day to judge myself for that.

I snuggled in and reveled in the small snow town splendor.

The Christmas Fair was full of delightful sights and smells. By far the most popular booth at the festival was *The Landers'* cookie booth. I caught sight of Carol's massive red beehive over the crowd. I squeezed in and blew a kiss to Carol and Ethel, who were surrounded by their fans.

Carol came over and gave me one of her bear hugs. She squeezed hard, and I let her. Ethel waved to me as I struggled for breath over her shoulder, and I smiled back at her. Of course, I bought some cookies when I was there.

Devlin looked down at me with the bag and arched one brow. "More *Marry Me Blueberry Crumble*?"

I croaked out a little odd laugh. "Just innocent cookies hopefully." I avoided his knowing eyes and looked around at anything but his hunky body in the flannel shirt and tight jeans.

He laughed at my un-comfortableness with his closeness. Jerk obviously knew the effect he had on women.

I searched for something to look at other than Devlin. One shop, in particular, caught my attention. It had handmade ornaments and natural-looking shirts and hoodies—just the kind of down-to-earth gifts I wanted to get for the over-indulged Somerset family.

I dragged Devlin over and perused the lovely organic goods. "Now these are the kind of ornaments we need to offset all the glitz of that Hollywood horror you call a Christmas tree."

"I'm sure our decorator would love that— shabby chic; emphasis on *shabby*."

I shushed him and held up one of the ornaments in the shape of a pine tree and admired it. "This is chic. This is where it's at, Devlin. Natural, not fake."

I glanced at the salesgirl's braids and dishwater blonde hair and yearned for my own locks that felt like real hair instead of hay.

I asked the girl, "Are these sweaters made from cotton?"

"Hemp, actually." She smiled back.

"Hemp? Wow, it feels great." I marveled.

"Yes, now it's legal again; we are one of the first farms in Vermont to switch over and grow hemp full time."

I admired the beauteous items. "Look, Devlin, how lovely." I elbowed him, and he sneered at me.

He looked at them reluctantly. "I guess they do have a certain homespun charm." He tossed his glorious mane, darn him, and said, "I prefer gold or silver–primarily platinum."

I looked at the girl. "We'll take all the ornaments you have and ten sweaters."

Devlin was chatting with neighbors and sipping on a hot chocolate. I held out my hand.

"What?"

"Credit card, honey?" I smiled, sugar-sweetly.

He raised his eyebrows and fished out his black and gold card with a grimace.

I shook my head. "Cheapo, stop acting like you're poor."

He snorted. "I'm not cheap."

I beamed as the girl put all of the items into boxes. I'd hope to teach the spoiled Somersets about the beauty of natural things and the true meaning of Christmas.

The young girl had almost finished packing the gifts into the bags when she said, "So many things we can make out of hemp now. We have a website if you want to check it out."

I nodded. "I will."

She continued, "Even these boxes are made of hemp." She packed an ornament into one.

I stopped. "Excuse me. What did you say?"

"These boxes." She pointed at my bag. "All of them are made of hemp."

I threw both my hands in the air and knocked Devlin's hot cocoa all over his camel coat.

He glared at me, and then stared down at the brown splotches that dappled his expensive coat.

"What's wrong with you?" he hissed like I was insane.

I waved a box in front of him.

"Hemp! Hemp! Hemp! Hemp! Hemp!"

I started jumping up and down and waving my hands and even threw in some twerking.

He pulled me to the side. "I'm sorry," he whispered to the girl. "Allie, settle down. People are looking."

"Devlin, don't you see? This is the answer! The answer to it all!"

Devlin did not see. He pointed to the spot on his coat. "This is Versace."

I waved away his stains and held up one of my packages and examined the box with glee. "I had forgotten all about hemp because it wasn't legal for so long and the import tax from Canada…"

Devlin glared at me.

"Hemp! "I screamed at him like he was deaf. He put a finger in his ear and shook his head.

"Devlin, this is it. I did my thesis on hemp. For every one acre of hemp, it takes five acres of trees to produce the same thing because it's a weed!"

Devlin rubbed his brow and looked around, embarrassed. "Let's go to the inn and get you a nice glass of wine; you're getting worked up." He pushed me toward *Wino's*, the local wine shop. I stuck my boot heels in.

"You don't see!" I looked up at him. "Hemp and wood both break down into cellulose—once that's done, *all the same machines, all the work, is the same.*"

I grabbed Devlin with both my hands. "I don't remember the exact numbers, but hemp is a fraction of the cost of trees to produce the same product—and better yet—*less* than plastic!"

Devlin's eyes widened. The possibilities were beginning to dawn on him.

"Less than plastic? Are you *sure*?"

I nodded like a bobble head out of control. "Yes! Cheaper than plastic bubble envelopes that pollute all the oceans and…"

He clapped his hand on my mouth, and I glared at him. He leaned in closer.

"You're saying if we make our boxes out of hemp instead of trees, we could undercut not only our box competition but plastic as well? Are you sure?"

I nodded and removed his hand. "Yes, without a doubt. And no jobs need to be lost! It might take a moment to transition over your fields from trees to fully hemp, but the workers and machines don't need any replacing! You could skyrocket Somerset Industries into the future as a worldwide leader in environmental packaging and beat all your competition!"

He looked at me intensely. "I'd have to see the numbers."

I nodded. "Of course."

"I have a team for that," he said as he stroked his cleft chin.

I dragged my eyes away from the cleft magnet and said, "It just might be enough of a new idea to win over your father."

A light went off in his eyes, and he nodded and smiled at me.

"It just might be at that."

Chapter 33

*I*t was a glorious night. The stars were shining, and there wasn't a cloud in the sky.

Devlin had hooked up an old-fashioned sleigh ride with a team of ponies, and he was riding them all about the property to the delight of the children.

I waved to them from the balcony, and they slid over the vast, snow-covered lawn, laughing and waving.

I planned to work on my formal dancing alone in the room while everyone was occupied. The constant acting job was wearing on me, and I needed some serious alone time.

I attempted to slip away and upstairs to our room when Sissy reached out and grabbed my hand. I hadn't even seen her lurking around the balcony, but she snuck up on me like a bad cold.

I smiled as sweetly as I could muster and said I was retiring, but she wasn't letting me get away. I glanced at Devlin driving the sleigh and wished I had gone along. Now I was stuck with Sissy.

She suggested we visit the stables while the rest of the family was busy. I couldn't figure out any way to get out of it, so I went along.

"I thought we might take a stroll on the horses together and...bond." But she cooed at me in lava tones. I didn't think that was such a great idea at all. I had visions of me feeding a carrot to Daisy and hightailing it back to my room ASAP.

We entered the stables, and the memories of riding and dancing with Devlin last night floated through my thoughts like a warm summer breeze. I guessed I might be able to handle a short walk on Daisy. Maybe Devlin would be impressed with my efforts?

Not that I cared.

Roy stepped out of his office and tipped his hat, and then his eyes widened when he saw it was the two of us. He looked back and forth between the horses and us.

"When Mrs. Albridge told me to saddle up the horses, I thought..." Roy stopped.

There were two massive thoroughbred horses saddled and ready to go. They snorted and stamped at the ground like rodeo bulls itching to get lose and gore someone.

I looked for an exit.

"Should I saddle up Daisy?" Roy asked uncertainly.

I nodded enthusiastically.

Sissy brushed his suggestion away. "Of course not. Daisy is for babies. Lightning and Gypsy will be perfect."

I gulped. Roy was making a tight line with his lips I didn't like at all.

Then Sissy's skinny talon was on my back, patting me awkwardly. "Let's ride and continue getting to know each other better."

I put on a practiced casualness. "Riding is really not my forte."

She raised a brow. "Big word for you, nice job."

I bit my lip. "Sure is snowy out," I hissed. Instead of beating her about the head with a stick. I looked around. Any stick would do.

Two hundred thousand dollars. Two hundred thousand dollars. Two hundred thousand dollars.

Gosh, darn it. I had to get out of this! These horses looked ready to run the Kentucky Derby! I doubted riding one of them would be anything like riding gentle Daisy. Escape plans drifted through my head. Heart attack? Important call? PMS?

Help!

I glanced at Sissy, and she was studying me like I was a biology experiment. "I know you from somewhere." She squeezed her eyes into tiny slits.

Code RED!

I dipped my head down to hide my Betty Boop googly eyes, because those I couldn't disguise. I focused on petting one of the horses instead, and it chomped at me nastily with its big horsey teeth. I pulled my hand back intact, luckily. *PMS it was.*

"You know, I'm really bloated." I made a face and grabbed my stomach. "Period pains."

Sissy smiled at me with a look that told me I wasn't pulling anything over on her. "Roy, be a good man and go fetch my Vicodin for Miss —"

She stopped. "You know, I don't believe you told me your last name. What is it?" She dropped the question like she had scored some point.

Shoot. Why the heck did Devlin and I not go over this? It seemed any conversation with Sissy was a ticking bomb waiting to explode. I hoped to goodness she wasn't tricking me and that she hadn't already quizzed Devlin. Gosh, darn her.

My heart beat fast, and I spit out my mom's maiden name. "Trudeau."

She raised one brow.

I realized at that moment that this little tete-a-tete at the stable was actually her way of cornering me into a private interrogation.

The horses snorted and pawed and Roy gestured with his hat. "They haven't been exercised since the heavy snow. Maybe I can take them out first and help let off some of their steam. Or I can saddle up some less feisty alternatives."

He looked down at me questioningly and then back at the spirited animals chewing on the bit behind him.

"These are perfect, Ray," Said Sissy.

"Roy," he corrected with a tip of his hat.

"She can ride Gypsy, Roy, and I'll ride Thunder."

"Lightning, you mean," said Roy, but Sissy didn't listen. "Devlin gushed about what an equestrian you were," She said.

I screwed up my face. Was she referring to Sofia? I wracked my memories and remembered some tabloid splashed across with the pair riding through central park on horses.

"I ..." I mumbled stupidly, trying to concoct a way to escape this. I had no idea Devlin had told her about ours or other relationships. Any moment alone with Sissy was dangerous. She seemed bent on proving that we were faking our love—and of course, she was right.

Sissy hoisted herself up onto her mountainous steed effortlessly and then leaned over and looked down at me like I was a peasant on the ground.

"Admit it. You and my brother concocted this whole charade."

I glanced at Roy, and he was staring at me with big *don't-do-it* eyes.

Right, Roy, I agree I sent him telepathically. Now if you could just turn around so I could grab her boot and body slam her to the floor like a hockey player that would be great. I'll take the penalty over riding the death beast.

"It's nothing personal, dear." Sissy just had to keep talking. "You're obviously not in our class – certainly not right for *my brother*. Why don't you tell me what service he bought you from? Escort? Fill in Secretary? Maid? Nothing personal."

I guess the gloves were off. Figuratively of course, because it was darn freezing and you bet I had on physical ones.

"Personal," I said with a toss of my new white straw hair. "How could I not take you telling me I'm pond scum personally?"

How dare she? If Sissy Somerset was going to poor shame me, I would be darned if she did it while she looked down at me from some stallion like the Queen of Sheba!

I glanced at the horses and then back at Roy. Even if I wanted to act cool, I didn't even know how to get up on a horse that giant. Thankfully, Roy saw my dilemma and rushed over to give me a leg up on the horse.

"Good luck," he whispered.

Soon I was eye to eye with my attacker.

I glanced down uneasily at the golden-colored horse moving about restlessly beneath me. I picked up the reins as Devlin had taught me and tried to calm myself. Well, I had the sitting thing down okay. I managed to straighten and put on my best Downton Abbey expression of haughty disdain.

"Money doesn't equate with class," I said. "And being able to ride around on some animal doesn't make you better than anyone else."

"Said the girl who can't ride," she spat back condescendingly.

My face flamed.

"Don't deny it," she laughed. "A ruse by my brother no doubt to make Father think you could ride. Part of your bigger plan to con my ailing father out of his own business. You should be ashamed of yourself, you social-climbing guttersnipe."

Guttersnipe?

Guttersnipe?

I looked at Roy, and he was shaking his head.

"Oooooh!" My mouth opened wide in anger. How dare that Sissy Somerset call me a guttersnipe!? It was on. Either I wrapped my hands around her neck, or I had to get away from her. I dug my heels into my horse in utter hubris and Gypsy sprang up with a leap and bolted straight out of the barn door.

The horse cantered down the snowy path a good quarter mile before I could slow her down to a trot.

"Whoa, whoa!" I said as I pulled back on the reins tightly. I was scared out of my mind. Daisy had been a rocking chair ride, but this wild thing was a Porsche!

I tried to hold her back, but she was pulling at the bit, wanting to run. I let up the reins just a tad, and Gypsy took off again and galloped at full speed down the trail.

I fought to keep my seat and grabbed fruitlessly for the saddle horn. But this was an English saddle that had no horns, or training wheels as I thought of it.

I grabbed on with my thighs and struggled to get the spirited horse under control. When a bunny popped out of the brush, Gypsy came to an abrupt stop and went straight up on two legs.

She halted so quickly, I nearly fell off. I scrambled back onto the seat and tried to regain my balance. I took a deep breath of relief and looked over my shoulder. Thankfully, Sissy hadn't seen my blundering. Maybe I had lost her. I looked around the dark pine forest. The moonlight filtered through the needles.

I took some controlled breaths and considered riding off behind the barn and hiding where Sissy couldn't find me. Maybe she would think I went ahead and I just keep going?

That's when I heard an ominous whistling through the pines. I felt the hair rise on my arms. Through the darkness

came a blood-curdling scream and the sound of flying
hoofs over hard snow.

I looked through the trees, trying to see what was
happening, when Sissy appeared like a banshee on her
black horse, galloping at top speed in my direction.

I didn't like the look of this.

My horse must have felt it too, because she started doing
this sidestepping nervous walk thing. Her eyes bulged,
and she threw her head back and forth, snorting and
pulling at the reins.

I pulled her back and held on tight. "It's okay, girl, just
hang on." I tried to calm her down, but my heart was
beating so hard, I could barely breathe.

Sissy approached us at full speed, and she swerved her
stallion to the side like a rodeo pro and rose up on two
legs, angrily pawing at the air in my direction. Gypsy
backed up in fear.

I don't know if it was because of the way the other horse
was jabbing his hoofs at us like Tyson, or the fact that Sissy
had this demented screwed-up prune face on that made
her look like *The Scream* painting.

She shrieked, "You wanna throw down with me, you
wanna be a Somerset? It's *on*!" With that, she pulled out
a whip with a barb at the end and slapped my poor
horse's butt wickedly hard.

Poor Gypsy leaped straight up in the air in pain and then
took off running up the trail into the dense, dark forest.

"Stop!" I screamed, 'Whoa!" The world was hurtling by in a blur of white and pines. We were going so fast, it was utterly out of control. I ducked and avoided the big branches I could make out in the dark, but I got whipped repeatedly by the smaller ones.

I was yelling, "Whoa! Whoa!" But the snapping twigs and thundering hooves drowned out my pleas. Somewhere along the way, I lost hold of the reins and grabbed onto Gypsy's mane and hung on for dear life.

Through the thick pines, in the distance, I saw a clearing, and Sissy was already there waiting.

"Help!" I screamed, as I burst into the clearing, still unable to stop the frightened horse.

Sissy gave a self-satisfied smirk when she saw my desperation and the horse out of control.

"The barn's right back there; it's hard to stop them when they know they're headed home." She dug both her heels into her horse with one nasty kick, and they raced off over the frozen field. Gypsy followed in their wake.

I spotted the bright red tip of the barn in the distance. We must have been going 60 miles an hour, and I prayed I wouldn't fall off until we made it back to the barn.

The barn was through the field, but it wasn't just a field. I blinked and focused ahead on what appeared to be a frozen stream. Rather than stopping, Sissy bolted right toward it!

What was she doing? Was this crazy loon going to kill us both? We couldn't run over that ice–I could already see thin puddles on the top.

Sissy turned and looked at me like Linda Blair out of *The Exorcist*, then spurred her horse on even faster toward the icy stream. With one final dig of her heels, Sissy and her horse sailed over the frigid river like Olympians.

I screamed, and suddenly we were racing through the air right behind them. Gypsy knew how to jump, thankfully, and she leaped effortlessly over the water and landed on the other side of the snowbank.

The only problem was that *I wasn't on the back when she landed.* I fell off in one horrible slow-motion moment. *Me bouncing out of the seat. Me catapulting through the air. Me landing on my butt, cracking the ice, and then the horrible revelation that I was sinking into the freezing water.*

The freezing water sent arrows of pain piercing through my entire body. I flailed and tried to pull myself off the edge with my wet gloves, but the ice broke around me in little fractures that spread like varicose veins.

"Sissy! Sissy!" I screamed. "Help!"

But Sissy was long gone. Gypsy was nowhere to be seen either—not that some horse could fish me out of my current dilemma.

I cried out again into the dark night, but there was no one there to hear. I gasped and struggled to pull myself onto the ice, but it kept breaking. I was so very, very cold, and my limbs felt weighted down. I pushed my arms to tread water, but I was getting tired.

I suddenly had the horrible revelation that I could die alone in this cold, watery death and never be found. I saw a branch, and I reached for it. I struggled to grasp the thin limb, giving thanks for trees and my life preserver, when I heard an ominous crack.

The branch broke under my pull, and I sank further beneath the cold, dark water. I fought with all my strength to swim back to the surface. I got my head above the water and sucked in a breath, but my arms were weak, and I found it harder to move to keep my head afloat.

I started to panic, and I swallowed some water and spat it out. I cried out again with all my strength. "Help me, please! Help me!"

I slid under the surface again, and blackness enveloped me. I felt myself sinking lower and lower.

When I started losing consciousness, I imagined I heard my name being called. Some inner survival mechanism kicked in and gave me hope. Though my arms were now useless, I fought with my last strength, kicking my legs as hard as I was able to so I could get to the surface.

"Here!" I screamed as I broke through the surface. I struggle to raise my hand up. "I'm here, help!"

"Allie!"

It was Devlin!

He was really there, not a mirage. I harnessed my last breath to call out.
"Devlin!"

Then I was dragged down again into the bitter cold and dark water. I felt myself sinking, and I had no energy left. I couldn't make my arms move, and I descended toward the bottom hopelessly.

And then I felt Devlin's hand grab mine. I numbly felt myself being pulled up and out of the water. I remember gasping for breath and the look of fear in Devlin's eyes, and then everything went black.

Chapter 34

1 awoke in delirium. My head was feverish, and the room dim. I felt the bed around me and opened my eyes.

A small group had gathered, and Carol Landers came over and picked up my hand as I fluttered into consciousness.

I focused on her kind face.

"What happened?"

She patted my hand. "It's okay, darling, you're going to be okay."

A man with a stethoscope appeared beside her. "This is my husband, Dr. Archibald." He stepped forward and smiled at me.

"It looks like the patient is better; how are you feeling, dear?"

Horrible, exhausted, and scared.

"I'm so confused."

"You fell in the water, honey. Nearly drowned, and Devlin pulled you out," said Carol.

"In the nick of time, I might add," clucked the old doctor. "One more minute and I'm not sure we could have gotten you back."

Jeeves, Mr. Somerset, and Alice stood at the back of the room, looking concerned.

I halfheartedly waved. Devlin was asleep on the settee at the end of the bed.

"Is he okay?"

I struggled to sit.

Dr. Archibald urged me back down. "Your fiancé is going to be okay, dear. He is getting some much-needed rest. He had his own battle with the ice before he was able to get you both out."

Mr. Somerset moved to his son's side. "I don't know how he managed to ride them both back to the house in the state we found them."

Carol patted Mr. Somerset on the back. "I think he is your son, with the fortitude to beat just about anything that comes his way."

Mr. Somerset nodded. "You're sure they don't need to be hospitalized, Dr. Archibald?"

"No, they're both past the worst of it. Just sleep and liquids at this point, and when they're ready, a good hearty meal.'"

Jeeves hustled to my side with some water and O.J.

"Should I bring food, miss?"

I shook my head. "No, thank you. But thank you all so much." I grabbed Jeeves's hand at his authentic look of concern.

The realization that I had nearly died was a lot to take along with my fever and shock. Dr. Archibald must have seen the weariness in my eyes, because he shuffled everyone out of the room.

He bent over and whispered, "I'll be back to check on you both. Sweet dreams, child."

Chapter 35

$\mathcal{I}$t was a restless night, broken up by nightmares and

thirst.

I felt a strong arm around me, and in the dim light, noticed Devlin lying beside me. He was sleeping soundly, and my eyes went wide, but I didn't move. His embrace felt so safe. His full lips parted as he slept.

He had saved me. The doctor said he had put himself in danger to save me. It was hard to hate him.

My head hurt, and figuring out my complicated feelings was too much to balance. How to fit Devlin into the slot of a jerk now?

The man I despised had risked his life for me. My ex-boyfriend wouldn't even give me a lift home during a blizzard.

I closed my eyes and snuggled into Devlin's arms.

I slept deeply through the rest of the night, and awoke in a warm haze, still clasped in Devlin's strong embrace. The morning sun had shined through the window and sent slanting shards of light across the room.

I froze when I realized Devlin was awake and stroking my hair. It felt so protective and loving, and I didn't move, not wanting to break the moment. There was a knock on the door. It was Jeeves with the doctor.

I looked over to see Devlin's eyes focused on me. I couldn't read them, but, for once, I dared to stare back into his beautiful gaze. He was stunningly handsome close-up.

"Come in, Jeeves, please," Devlin said in a deep morning voice. He smiled and gave me a quick hug as he gently detangled his arms from my body.

I blushed and felt myself getting heated, but it wasn't a fever.

Chapter 36

$\mathcal{D}$r. Archibald gave us both a clean bill of health. The Mistletoe Ball was tonight, and we had been cleared to go if we rested all day.

I could hardly believe it was Christmas Eve, and my heart hurt for my own home. I wondered what my father was doing right now.

Devlin and I were alone in the room, and I was glad I didn't have to deal with anyone else. He was bare-chested, clad only in black silk pajama pants. He was pacing, as usual, in front of the fireplace, and it was hard to not stare at his perfect physique.

He had been so concerned and loving, but now he was back in his head.

"Look, Allie, this is a significant event tonight. I think if we get through this, we're through the woods."

I smiled slowly. Back to the facts, ma'am. We got a job to do. Part of me felt hollow and yearned to have him back in bed next to me. It had been so long since I had someone hug me or stroke my hair. I had thought I was immune to men at this point, but now I wasn't so sure. My single rock status was melting into mush with each move of that muscled chest.

I pulled my eyes away and focused on eating. Devlin seemed to have recovered nicely as he was still pacing, which resembled exercise.

I took a slug of my chocolate milk and watched the show.

"Your only job is to look beautiful and look in love with me. I will announce to everyone that we're getting engaged, and then it will be official."

I gulped. "Okay."

He glanced at me. "Just remember not to say much. We're almost there, and—"

"The snow looks extra white tonight." I smiled dumbly.

He gave me a thumbs-up. "That's perfect."

I felt my heart lurch and brought my hand to my stomach.

"Are you okay?" He looked concerned.

I waved it off. "Just weak – more food." I stuffed a croissant in my mouth to avoid sticking my foot in it. I was happy this charade was coming to an end.

Devlin observed me as he paced. "Sissy's been oddly quiet. I'm not sure if she has something up her sleeve."

"Maybe she's hiding because she almost killed me," I said, chewing on my pastry.

"She…what?"

"She plotted to get me in that water. She got me on Gypsy and kept going when I fell."

Devlin froze. His skin paled. But he believed me. "We have to be on guard."

I took a deep breath and cleared my throat. "Devlin…" His name sounded different in my mouth now. Not like something I wanted to gag up, more like a soft kitten purr. "I think you should talk to your father."

He rolled his eyes. "I've been talking to my father."

"I mean, *honestly*. Tell him the truth about us– tell him everything."

Devlin's aristocratic dark eyebrows shot up. "Is your temperature up again? There is no way I can tell my father I brought the chauffeur's daughter here to pose as my fiancé so I could trick him into signing over what I wanted." He choked out a rough laugh. "That is exactly what Sissy would love. She'd win. It would be over, and Somerset Industries will be a thing of the past."

I continued to unabashedly stare at Devlin as he moved like a great cat in the zoo, prancing back and forth with his muscular body. That body that was curled up next to me just hours ago.

I bit into my croissant and hoped I didn't have crumbs on my mouth. Then I took a sip of coffee.

"I don't know a lot about life, Devlin, and I'm not super smart. I'm not a successful businessperson like you are, and I haven't been around the world or speak multiple languages like you do—which is very cool, by the way."

Devlin's eyebrows went up.

"But we are the same in some ways. Both of us lost people we love too soon."

He looked at me with a new seriousness.

"There were so many things that I wish I would have said to my mother even though I had time. But once she was gone, I realized there was so much I never said…How much I loved her, how much I appreciated her, how much I looked forward to every day, taking it for granted that she would be there like the sun, every morning shining down on my life—and then she wasn't."

Tears filled my eyes, and Devlin came over and brought me a tissue. He handed me the box.

"Let's not go getting all morose—you're going to swell your eyes up, and you'll never get your makeup to cover that." He patted me awkwardly on the back and then cleared his throat.

"Come, now. Cheer up and look like a future Somerset. We don't cry."

I sob-laughed at him even harder. He sat down on the bed next to me and used his thumb to wipe away a tear gently.

I stared into his eyes. "Your father is almost 90. You still have a chance to fix things with him. Tell him you love him. Tell him what you've gone through to try and prove yourself to him, and how much you need his approval."

Devlin shook his head adamantly.

I got up out of bed and pulled my Zsa Zsa Gabor nightgown around myself, self-consciously. The morning light shone through the ethereal fabric, and I'm pretty sure it was see-through…

I grabbed his hands. "Have no regrets, Devlin."

I shook his hands up and down to capture his attention. He looked me in the eye.

"You never know in life if you'll see someone again. There are no guarantees. You didn't get that chance with your mother, and you're still hurt by that…"

He opened his mouth to disagree, but I put my finger to his luscious lips and stopped him. "You're lying to your dad. You don't have to. Talk to him; tell him you love him, and how much you want to save his legacy. Just tell him the truth, Devlin. No regrets."

Devlin took a deep inhalation as if he'd sucked in my meaning, and he moved to the window and opened the curtains to stare out at the mountains. When he turned back to me, his eyes were clouded over, our moment of closeness gone.

"I'm going to take my father early to get his tux tailored.
Are you going to be okay meeting me at the ball? Jeeves
will escort you over, of course."

I nodded. "I'll be ready."

"Okay." He slipped out of his pajama pants in one fluid
movement and stood naked except for his form-fitting
underwear.

I blushed. But kept looking.

He didn't notice my red flaming face, thankfully.

"I don't want to put any undue pressure on you, but some
of the wealthiest and titled people from all over the world
will be in attendance tonight. Especially now that the
planes are cleared to fly again." He slipped on a pair of
grey fitted slacks that melted around his body like butter.
He followed it with a light blue shirt and ran his hand
through his hair. He looked better than my croissant,
which was saying a lot.

I stuttered. "What should I wear?"

Devlin adjusted his tie in the mirror.

"I bought you a dress, so you'll look like a queen– as
befitting my fiancé." He strode toward the door with a
determined look, and then stopped.

"We just have to get through tonight, Allie, and we'll
both get what we want."

He winked at me and shut the door.

Chapter 37

$\mathcal{I}$t was nearing time for the ball, and I was ready, but

nervous. I touched my hair, which I had styled with soft beach waves. My long locks now hung down in spiral mermaid curls to my waist, and for the first time, I thought maybe the blonde worked on me after all. That said, I couldn't wait to strip hair back to its natural color as soon as I got home.

   Tonight's Mistletoe Ball rang through my head, bringing fairytale images to mind.

I was excited for Devlin to see me all dressed up. He had picked out a beautiful cherry red dress and had sent a wrist corsage in matching red roses.

I looked down at the pretty flowers I wore as a bracelet. Roses. I inhaled the lovely fragrance. Maybe Devlin did listen to some of the things I said? Most likely not. I still yearned for his approval for some reason, but I told myself I just wanted to fulfill my side of the deal successfully.

My makeup and hair were done; I wrapped my silk robe around me and came out of the powder room humming. I stopped short when I saw Sissy in my room, casually going through my closet as if she owned it.

I inhaled deeply and scanned the room, hoping Devlin was there for support and protection, but I knew he was with his father and had planned to meet me at the ball.

That meant I was alone with Satan.

Sissy looked me over. "I am sorry about last night. In all fairness, you didn't have to ride if you didn't know how to keep your seat." She shrugged her shoulders. "Crazy to get on a mount like Gypsy if you weren't an advanced rider."

I wanted her out of my room. *Our room.* Now.

Sissy pulled out my red ballgown with one of her claws. My shoulders tensed. I didn't like seeing it in her demon grasp.

"My, my, this looks like a Halston." She fingered the stunning red gown with the plunging neckline. I took in how low it went and gulped. I hoped ribs were attractive, because I certainly didn't have any cleavage to fill that.

She was running her hands through it and turning it back and forth. I wanted to snatch it away from her, but with my luck, it would have ripped.

"St. Lauren? Chanel?" She examined the tag. I willed her to return it to the closet, and reluctantly she gave in to my Spock mental demands.

"Devlin bought it," I said, when it was safely back in the wardrobe. "He's got better taste than I do."

Sissy laughed. "He's got better taste than most of us."

I glanced at my closet and wondered why she had been going through my things? That's when I noticed my chauffeur outfit, peaking out of my backpack that I had shoved in the corner.

I froze, and slowly moved over and positioned myself in front of the revealing evidence. Sissy continued rifling through my dresses as if she were buying something.

"So, the big Ball—you'll be introduced to everyone that is anyone. Your engagement news will be official."

I looked down at Sofia's enormous ring on my finger. Official. Last act. I had to get her out of here.

"Just so I can tell all our friends, or should I say my brother's ex's...."

I half shut the French door of the closet..

"*Exactly how* did you get my commitment-phobic brother to agree to marry you when every other girlfriend he's ever had never succeeded?"

I smiled uncomfortably.

"Lucky, I guess."

She squinted at me with her freaky contact eyes.

"I still feel like I've seen you somewhere before," she said.

I shrugged uncomfortably under her scrutiny and started flapping my hands in a shooing motion. As if I was herding some cattle out of the field.

"Well, you better get along, Sissy. I need to finish getting ready. Wash my pits, you know?"

She made a face.

I went for the gross-out, which actually works well in getting people to leave.

She looked suspiciously at me and then back at the closet, as if she knew she was missing something.

Jeeves broke the tension when he knocked, and he let himself in through the cracked door with an ice bucket and champagne.

Sissy plopped her skinny butt down on the bed and motioned for Jeeves to bring a glass to her at her new post.

"Oh, I don't need to hurry off," she drawled. "I thought we'd bury the hatchet. I'm glad to see you looking well."

I bit my lip. *No thanks to you.* She had left me to die.

I tight smiled.

"Well, thanks for checking on me," I lied. "But I really do have so much to do before the ball. Shouldn't you be getting ready?"

Sissy drank her glass of champagne as if she had all the time in the world. She perched on our big bed and studied me as she swallowed.

I glanced at her, but all I could see were images of Devlin's warm body, and mine nestled into that big love bed. I tore my gaze away when I heard a loud *bang!*

We all turned to see the bedroom door fling wide open, and Sissy's two giant white poodles came stampeding into the room.

Of course, they leaped all over me, leaving little tear marks all over my new robe.

I looked down, dismayed.

Jeeves came over to help me, but I noticed one of the dogs had got into the closet and was pulling my chauffeur uniform out of the back!

I ran over and stuck my foot on the uniform and tried to shut the door.

I should have known I was no match for two giant poodles.

Before I knew it, they gang-jumped me and knocked me over. I lost my balance, and as I desperately grasped for something to stop my fall, I toppled most of the hangers from my closet and took them down with me in a blaze of designer duds. I landed with a thump on the expensive Persian rug.

Jeeves was beside himself trying to shoo them out, but they had doubled down on dog crazy and were barking and running around the suite out of control.

I glanced fearfully back at the closet–but my uniform was safely out of sight for now. Phew.

I crawled over to the closet on all fours and attempted to retrieve my new clothes that were now littered all over the floor.

I heard growling and looked over to see the poodles having an all-out tug-of-war with my red ball gown!

I jumped up to my feet like Olga Korbit.

"No! Oh, no!" I prayed to God they wouldn't rip it." Sissy, help!"

She sipped her champagne from the bed like she was watching a reality TV show. Jeeves rushed over to my aid, but it was too late.

An eerie *RIPPPPPPPPPP!* resounded through the room *and my ball gown tore right in half.*

I closed my eyes, moaned, and blew out my breath.

Each of the poodles now held half my dress in their mouths triumphantly. The bright red fragments draped from their canines.

Sissy clapped her hands, and the two poodles jumped to obey her. They spat out the remnants of my dead gown on the floor and sat upright like perfect soldiers on command, looking at Sissy for their next move.

I looked from them to her.

"Are you kidding me? You could have just clapped your darn hands? What? Why?"

Sissy sauntered out of the room with a self-satisfied smirk and the dogs at her heels.

"See you at the ball."

Chapter 38

1 caught up to Sissy just as she was almost out of the door. I stepped on her flared pant bottom, and she fell back into my room flat on her back.

She looked up at me like a fish I had pulled out and flung on my boat.

I straddled her and motioned for Jeeves to leave the scene. He rushed out and shut the door.

I looked down at Sissy sprawled on the ground and saw the fear in her eyes. Good. She *should* be afraid.

I pointed my finger in her face. "I know you are undermining Devlin and I know you are lying about your father."

She tried to struggle up, but I dropped to my knees and pinned down both her arms.

"And you almost killed me."

Sissy went to open her mouth, and I dead-eyed her. "Don't you dare," I hissed out in my best Slytherin imitation. "Here's the deal. I'm done with your rotten spoiled attitude. If you do one more thing to Devlin or me, I swear you will not believe the Stephen King horror I am capable of releasing." I double pointed to my big googly eyes.

She struggled again, and I glared at her with said crazy eyes. "Don't forget. *I'm from Jersey.*"

I let her go, and she scampered out of the room. My breath whistled out in a low rumble and I shut the door with a slam for effect. Well that was classy. Pinning my fake fiancé's sister to the ground like I was Hulk Hogan. In my defense, I'm pretty sure there wasn't any instruction on how to deal with an evil sister in the etiquette videos.

******

I had no idea what I was going to do. I held up the two pieces of the gown like they were kryptonite and showed them to Chef Pierre in the kitchen.

He wiped his hands on his apron and looked at me with a sad face. "Ooh, la la! What has happened here?" He said in his heavy French accent.

"Poodles."

Just then, the twin poodles came running through the kitchen with Sissy's youngest son, Adam. They squealed and romped.

Pierre looked at the dogs. "I see."

"Devlin picked it out special. Do you think Mrs. Albright might be able to work some of her sewing magic?"

Mrs. Albright had been with the Somersets as long as Jeeves. She oversaw the maids and seemed able to cope with any problem. I wondered if she had a miracle in her pocket for me.

"I hope so, *Chérie*," he said, looking at the ripped pieces and shaking his head. "Ooh, and Halston, too…my favorite."

Mrs. Albright was in the utility room overseeing the laundry when I came in with my mopey face, and she turned to me with her brows knit.

"What's wrong?"

Pierre and I each held up a piece of the ripped gown. She brought both her hands to her face and shook her head.

"I'll do my best, miss" she said, looking back and forth between the two pieces of my dress.

Just then, I caught sight of a bright red tower bobbing happily down the hall. It belonged to none other than Carol Landers. She was making her way toward us with her red beehive waving back and forth jauntily. It was nice to see her friendly face.

"Oh, sorry to interrupt you all, but we left some of our rolling pins here, and Ethel's having a conniption. I thought I'd stop over pick them up before she complained all through Christmas morning." She smiled brightly.

"Good to see you up and about, doing well, Allie. Devlin well?"

I nodded.

"Yes. Thank you, Carol, and to your husband, Dr. Archibald. You are both so kind."

She glanced at the dress and Mrs. Albright in front of the sewing machine shaking her head.

"Doing some sewing?"

"Not exactly," I said. "More like mending."

She took in the situation, and Carol's eyebrows rose. "Oh my, I see there's been a death in the family."

I nodded. "It was my gown for tonight; I don't have the heart to tell Devlin that I don't have anything suitable to wear to the Mistletoe Ball. It means so much to him."

Aunt Carol picked up the house phone to make a call. "I think I might be able to help you.

Chapter 39

*C*arol's niece hugged us and welcomed us into her cozy household.

Her lovely home was filled with Christmas delights. The aroma of cookies baking and the homemade Christmas decorations felt like a beam of sunshine in the middle of winter.

The beautiful woman sat us down and went to the kitchen to grab some spiced cider she had made.

"Your niece is Summer Landers?" I whispered to Carol.

She nodded. "Summer Anderson now."

I recognized Summer Landers *Anderson* from her makeup billboards, commercials, and, of course, her famous Sports Illustrated covers.

She was beaming that star smile at us now as she returned with our cider and juggled an adorable baby at her hip. The infant had big blue eyes and tufts of white hair. I couldn't help but think how Devlin's hair had been that color when he was a child. Now it was raven black–I stopped myself from dwelling on Devlin and children and focused on my plight.

"My Aunt Carol says you're in need of a fairy godmother?" Summer smiled at me kindly.

I looked at them, confused.

Summer set a plate of cookies in front of us. "A dance to go to and no dress? That is a problem."

"Actually, it's a super fancy ball." I frowned.

"Oooh, then we need a ballgown!" Her stunning blue eyes opened wide.

Summer winked at her aunt.

"You've come to the right place."

She looked me over quickly. "Size Two?"

I nodded.

Within moments, Summer glided out of the room and returned with a dress on a hanger, a clear protector over it.

"I think this will do nicely. They let me keep a lot of the outfits from my shoot. It's a Vanderloo."

I had no idea who *Vanderloo* was, but I knew I was in heaven when I put on that dress.

I spun around in the mirror, and the gown floated about me like golden clouds and swirls of cream meringue.

I stood in front of the mirror and marveled at myself. It was like a dream—or someone else's life. I reached up and touched my cascading locks and the golden sash that highlighted my waist.

When I moved, little sequins of lights bounced everywhere. I had never looked this good in my life.

My light hair with this cream gown looked angelic, and when I moved, it sent out golden stardust and sparkles.

I gasped. "I can't believe how beautiful this is! Thank you so very much!"

Carol and Summer were all smiles. Carol put a finger to her mouth and glanced at Summer. "It's missing something, don't you think?"

I glanced at the mirror. I looked good to me.

I heard somebody bounding up the stairs and turned to see Ethel Landers appear breathless at the door.

"I brought it!" she said triumphantly as she held up a tiara in her hand.

Ethel came over and placed it on my head.

The tiara was delicate and simple, and it was sprinkled with diamonds.

I caught my breath. I turned to the group for approval, and the three Landers ladies clapped with glee.

Carol smiled. "Oh my, it's a good thing Devlin is already in love with you, because if he weren't, I swear he would drop down on his knee tonight after seeing you!"

Devlin on his knee.

That made me smile.

The arrogant sexiest man of the year groveling at my slippers. It was a delicious thought.

Chapter 40

*E*thel glanced at the time and clapped her hands as if

she were a coach.

"Okay, gang. We have to get moving and go over and
help Dodie at the cookie contest before she gets
swarmed." She turned to me. "And it's time for you to get
to the ball. Do you have everything, darling?"

I looked at my fairy godmothers. "I can't thank you
enough. But I do have one last favor. Do you think you can
drop me back at the Chalet on the way? We came in the
bakery van and..."

Ethel waved a hand. "Oh, darling, we've got that covered. You are *not going to the Mistletoe Ball in that dress in our bakery van!*"

I looked at Summer and Carol, and they were shaking their heads and smiling mischievously.

Suddenly, there was a knock at the door, and Summer opened it.

A young couple stood dressed in matching old-fashioned coachmen outfits. The young man bowed. "Your chariot awaits."

My mouth dropped, and Devlin wasn't here to close it. Ethel clapped me on the back "We couldn't find a pumpkin at such short notice, but I could find my daughter-in-law Elle and her husband Dayton who happen to run the stables up at Eagle's Point."

Behind the couple waited a stunning white carriage rimmed in gold and twinkly lights. Attached to it were four white horses with golden bridals and festive red plumes shooting out of their headgear. I gasped and brought my hands to my face.

"Don't cry!" Ethel said. "You'll ruin your makeup!"

I choked back the tears, remembering Devlin saying the same thing.

She wrapped me in a big embrace. "You're going to be the belle of the ball, Allie."

I held on tight, and it felt good to hug her. It was amazing what good friends they had become in such a short while. I looked past Ethel at the Cinderella sleigh and felt as if I were sleepwalking in a dream. This was the kind of stuff that happened to other girls—not to me. I was just a girl from Jersey trying to save some trees.

Dayton held his hand out to escort me, and Summer draped a *fake* white fur stole around me at the last minute and gave me a reassuring pat.

I slipped into the magical carriage and settled into the red seat. Is this how Meghan Markle felt? I looked back at the Landers and waved.

I wiped away a lone tear with the handkerchief Ethel had slipped me. I was playing the perfect part of a fairytale princess, but I was the only one that knew this wasn't a fairytale, *it was a lie.*

Tomorrow when I woke, this game was all going to be over. I'd go home to Jersey, and Devlin and I would never have any reason to talk again.

I took a deep breath and looked down at my sparkling gown. But it wasn't going to be over until I made a heck of a splash at the Mistletoe Ball.

Chapter 41

*T*he ballroom was exquisite. I had watched the goings-on from my window as a child, but now I was here. It was like falling into a fantasy movie.

I gazed around at the splendor and glitz and the stately guests dressed in sleek low cutting gowns much like the chic dress Devlin had initially picked out for me.

All the men were stunning in their tuxes. Mistletoe hung from the rafters, and a full orchestra played from the side.

Jeeves rang a golden bell and beamed at me. "Miss Allie of New Jersey!" he called out to the crowd, announcing my arrival.

The crowd turned as one and looked at me.

I lifted my head as I entered the room. The crowd began to murmur. I felt a blush creep up as people stopped talking and stared at me.

I smiled and cast my eyes about, looking for Devlin. I spotted him next to his father in deep conversation. He looked up, drawn by the buzz, and his eyes opened wide.

He sauntered across the ballroom with a smile on his face.

He slowly perused me with his gaze. I took a deep breath. I hoped I made him proud.

He held out his hand. I realized everyone had stopped talking and were looking at us. I gulped.

Devlin leaned in and whispered,

"We are the guests of honor as we are announcing our engagement." He winked at me. "It's a tradition; we dance first."

I looked around the room, and my head was swimming. Diamonds, gowns, servants, flowers. Devlin took my hand and led me onto the dance floor and pulled me close.

"Breathe, Allie. Breathe." I tried. "Just lean into me and remember what we practiced." I clung to him gladly.

"I'm sorry about the dress you picked out for me," I mumbled as the music started and he embraced me tighter.

"You look amazing," he whispered in my ear, like a caress. I blushed and swallowed. Why was it suddenly so important what Devlin Somerset thought of me? Darn tree killer.

The chandelier light bounced off the ceiling, and my dress, as Devlin swirled me around expertly.

"You're doing great, Allie," he said, and beamed at me with a genuine smile.

I caught my breath and avoided his eyes. This was making me feel something odd. My stomach felt rumbly, and I was finding it hard to speak. I put my head on his shoulder and moved with the dance.

I was still in a daze when the music ended, and Devlin pulled back to gaze into my eyes.

"I have wonderful news, Allie. And it's all because of you."

Allie. The way he said my name, like an embrace instead of an insult. I looked up at him. It must have been the lights, but he was looking at me differently.

"So, you found a new dress." Sissy's icy voice cut in like a dagger. I dropped Devlin's hands, and the moment was gone. Lord, it was Christmas. Help me be forgiving.

"Too bad it's not at all in fashion this season," Sissy continued.

Carol Landers and Dr. Archibald appeared out of nowhere just in time to hear Sissy's barb. I breathed a sigh of relief to see their kind faces.

Carol made a big to-do about me, as if she hadn't been there the whole time I was dressing.

"You look stunning, Allie. Your hair, that dress– dare I say, is that a Vanderloo?"

Sissy gasped and leaned over to look closer.

"A *Vanderloo?*" She stared at my dress in awe. "I've been on his waiting list for five years!"

She eyed me up and down with new respect, and Carol winked.

Devlin waved to the orchestra, and they began playing a new song.

"Excuse me," he said to the group. "But I think this is our dance, darling." He held out his arm for me.

Anything to get away from Sissy. I waved to Carol and the doctor and planted myself securely in Devlin's arms.

He swept me into the center of the exquisite ballroom and whisked me about the room to the beautiful tune. "I love this music," I began to say, and then it dawned on me. I knew this song. I looked up at Devlin, and he was smiling at me.

"Is this from the *Rogers & Hammerstein's Cinderella* soundtrack?"

Devlin nodded.

"I thought you hated this," I said.
"You love it, though, right?"

I nodded, confused. *As if he'd ever cared what I wanted before.*

Devlin was the picture of a gallant gentleman as he twirled me about the dance floor like a pro. My dress billowed around me, and I felt like a princess.
"I have wonderful news, Allie, and it's all because of you." He beamed his dynamic smile at me and pulled me in close, then dipped me backward dramatically. I caught my breath and was thankful I took those yoga classes that allowed me to be contorted like this without passing gas.

His gray eyes bore into mine.
"I can't tell you how happy you've made me, and I can't wait to share the news with you when we're alone." He squeezed both my hands, and I couldn't help but smile ear to ear. "Now I want to make you happy. I requested this song, especially for you."
With that, Devlin twirled me around, and my dress floated around me like a cloud. I had never felt so beautiful. He held me close and expertly maneuvered us around the dance floor and away from the staring crowd and out onto the veranda.
Outside, we were alone with the stars.

It was a winter wonderland of lights and snow. Fire torches dotted the perimeter to ward off the chill, and twinkly lights hung from them. It was stunning.

I looked around us. "This is breathtaking."

"You're breathtaking," Devlin said, as he slid his strong arm tighter around my waist. His legs were pressed to mine, and I was finding it hard to think or breathe. His hand on my back, the stars overhead, it seemed like a fairytale come true.

We looked into each other's eyes, and we danced. With the moon and the stars and my heart beating so wildly, it made me wish I had done more cardio at the gym.

His smile shone, and he spun me in circles and gazed in my eyes, and I closed my eyes and smiled as I listened to the romantic song of true love.

That's when the night was sliced by some of the worst off-tune singing I'd ever heard. Would it be cliché to say that, nonetheless, it was music to my ears?

"*Ten minutes ago, I saw you. I looked up when you came into the room. It gave me the feeling the room had no ceiling or floor.*" Devlin half sang it in my ear along with the music.

I pulled back and laughed at him.

"Let me tell you something, Devlin. You don't have to whisk me off my feet. I'm a sure deal; you paid for me."

He bowed dramatically. "I did."

He spun me around in a circle, singing and laughing. I'd never seen this carefree and joyous side of him.

He threw open his arms.

"*I have found her!*" He sang loudly, and out of tune.

"*I have found him!*" I returned, equally as dramatically, throwing my arms in the air. "He's *the light of the star of my eyes.*"

"*We are dancing…*" Devlin took my hands in his and spun me around again in a circle of stars and laughter.

"*We are flying…*" I sang breathily.

"*And she's taking me back to the sky.*"

He pulled me in close, and his eyes sparkled with the light of the candles and my diamond tiara. I felt myself go cold with fear and hot with fever at the same time. Like when your temperature is so high, you can't decide if you're sweating or freezing. I had to get out of here.

This was too dreamy for me. This feeling was exactly what I wanted to stay away from. I knew how love went. Love started like *this* and went straight to two gallons of Rocky Road and a carton of tissues. *What goes up must come down.* There was no escaping physics except in my fantasies.

Devlin was staring at me now as if reading my mind. He hugged me to him closer, and I felt safe and scared all at once.

"You're not singing your part," he teased softly into my ear.

"I'm not," I said stupidly.

I didn't know what I felt except that I didn't want this moment to stop. If I could just freeze a moment and keep it safe forever. *If only.*

He sang into my ear again. "*In the arms of my love, I'm flying over mountain and meadow and glen, and I like it so well that for all I can tell I may never come back to Earth again...*" He pulled back and took both my hands and looked at me tenderly.

"*We may never come back to Earth again.*" We sang the last part together.

He hit the last high note off tune on purpose, and we both burst out laughing. He was doing such an excellent job of faking as if he liked me, I almost believed it!

I looked around, suddenly self-conscious of our bubble of closeness, expecting to see Mr. Somerset in the corner witnessing this romantic display as proof of our devotion. Devlin was smart like that. But we were alone.

I realized that this show had been for me, and I caught my breath. I didn't understand until strong, forceful arms pulled me into a passionate embrace.

Soft, sure lips found mine. I kissed Devlin back with abandon and melted against him.

I had never felt so enchanted as I did in this magical moment. Time went by, but I would have never known. My world was filled with gray eyes and full lips and the feel of every bit of Devlin Somerset pressing up against me.

"How miraculous that I would find you. Where were you hiding my whole life, little one?" He put my face in his hands and kissed me again, long and hard—*and on purpose.* When he pulled back from me, I almost fell into the pool of him. That's when Sofia screamed.

"*Devlin!* What is the meaning of this?"

Her shrill voice cut through the air like a chainsaw breaking our precious bubble.

We broke away from each other and looked at the small crowd that had made its way out onto the veranda to witness the scene. My face flamed with guilt as soon as I recognized her.

Sofia Denario looked AMAZING! Of course.

She was dressed in all red and looked like the darn bombshell she was. She had diamonds draped all over her, except for one noticeably naked finger.

I instinctively stuck my hands behind my back and tried to shrink up to a smaller, less noticeable size of myself like Fred Flintstone when he wanted to disappear.

More people had made their way onto the balcony. Sissy headed the group. She looked at me with her scary fake contacts. She had a self-satisfied look on her face, and I saw Devlin's father was behind her with a sad expression.

I let out a deep breath. This was worse than any nightmare I had imagined when I went over my list of worst-case scenarios. This level of nuclear disaster at Mr.

Somerset's special Mistletoe Ball had not even been on the list. This could not have been any worse.

And then I saw the paparazzi—and of course, that was worse.

I slapped my hand to my head and left it there to shield myself from the photographers and hoped to goodness my white hair and fancy getup made me unrecognizable to anyone that might see me on TV.

How would I explain this to my father? I had only told him that I had to stay four days, not any details. And my friends? Or worse yet, how to explain to *The Tree Lovers Coalition* about cavorting with the worst of our enemies?

"Devlin! How could you leave me?" Sofia raged, encouraged by the publicity. She began cursing in Spanish, and her hands were flying around at hyper speed, so she looked like she was in a Karate competition. Lights popped, and the cameras clicked, documenting every bit of the show.

Devlin's mouth flew open in surprise. He looked back and forth between Sissy and Sofia.

"Sofia? How did you know where I lived—how did you get here?" Devlin sputtered.

His eyes met Sissy's, and he shook his head.

Suddenly, Sofia screamed at the top of her lungs like she was being bludgeoned, which I must admit I might have considered if the darn cheese knife wasn't so dull.

"You!? You?!" she shrieked, pointing at me.

Sofia's large lips opened. "I know you! You're the unattractive lady chauffeur who drove us."

I wished I could have sunk through the floor.

Sissy snorted out a triumphant laugh. "I knew it."

Now Sofia was jumping up and down, flapping every extremity she had in a full-blown Latina breakdown. I was hoping she might blow her top right out of there and fly away, but no.

She turned to Devlin and shouted amidst more rapid hand waving.

"Why is the chauffeur wearing my ring!?"

She lunged over and grabbed my hand from behind my back. I yelped as she started tugging at the huge diamond on my finger. I looked around in shock as she jerked my arm around in an unsuccessful attempt to yank it off my hand. She obviously didn't know how much I bloated when I ate cheese. My lactose induced fat knuckle would not yield.

All the guests stood mute in witness to this embarrassing debacle. Some of them helped themselves to the lavish buffet while they watched the drama unfold.

Devlin had his arms around Sofia's waist, trying to pull her off me, and Sofia had my wrist in a death grip and was violently twisting the ring back and forth in an attempt to free it from the fat knuckle.

"Mine! Fake! Fraud!" Sofia railed as she tugged on the unyielding engagement ring.

"Oww! Oww!" I said, pulling my hand back.

She stamped her feet in double time, throwing a fit. She threw her arms in the air and stared at the heavens.

"Why, Devlin, why?"

Neither God nor Devlin bothered to answer, but a stunning redhead stepped forward and said,

"I assume the same reason *Devlin asked me to be his last-minute date.* What is going on here, Devlin?"

The crowd turned to look at the newcomer.

Devlin looked like he'd seen a ghost.

"Vanessa? What are you doing here?" His voice cracked.

She stepped onto the stage and cast a disparaging look at Sofia and me. Sofia had stopped pulling at my finger long enough to take in the new beautiful woman admonishing Devlin.

"You did call me and ask me to be your date. Or fake fiancé. Didn't you?"

Devlin wiped his brow, and his father frowned. "Yes but, that was before..." He glanced at Sofia, who now had her big red lips around my finger, sucking on the ring in an attempt to lubricate it over the fat knuckle.

Gross.

I didn't want Sofia's huge fake collagen-pumped lips on my digits. I tried to shake her off, but she had suction like a Hoover.

My eyes met Devlin's. Devlin's eyes suddenly glazed over as another beautiful girl with black hair to her waist pushed through the crowd. She stopped in front of the others and looked at Devlin with her hands on her hips.

"And you called me as well, Devlin Somerset. Why don't you let us know what kind of game you're playing?"

Devlin ran his hands through his hair and let out his breath, but the trick didn't seem to work this time.

"Estella."

He turned back and forth like a deer caught in the headlights, unsure what to say. His eyes met mine again. The camera clicking was deafening, and the bright lights nearly blinded me as the paparazzi had a field day.

There was no midnight bell ringing, but I knew when it was time for a quick exit. I pulled my finger out of Sofia's mouth and pushed her off me. I grabbed that ring, and I heaved the massive diamond off with one last painful tug over the fat knuckle. I handed it to Sofia triumphantly.

She looked down at it. "I loosened it up," she said matter-of-factly as she slipped it on her finger.

Devlin called out to the photographers. "Please, gentlemen, this is a special ball in honor of my deceased mother. I will ask you all to please take your footage and story and leave."

He waved his hand, and a group of servants appeared like a small army around the paparazzi and herded them out.

Sissy's eyes were gleaming like Snidely Whiplash throwing a poor family from their home. She had planned this whole torrid reveal, and she was enjoying every minute. Her mouth was pulled tight in a freaky smug smile.

The paparazzi and most of the crowd were finally ushered off the balcony when I caught Mr. Somerset's eyes.

I swallowed and mouthed, "I'm so sorry."

Chapter 42

I don't know what Mr. Somerset thought, but I could

imagine how much I had fallen in his esteem. A true frog. I couldn't bear to think about it. I had lied to a good person because I needed money—even if it was for a worthy cause. Our folly had blown up in our face, and it was time to exit stage right. I had to get out of there, and fast. But before I went, I was taking Sissy down with me.

I've watched my share of horror films, and the heartless killers often begin as an average person that has been pushed too far.

Past the point of no return.

Past all forgiveness.

Past the point of faking or caring.

These are the crazies you really have to fear, because you know they have nothing to lose and thus anything goes. Head spinning. Projectile puking or possibly being able to set someone's entire body on fire just by the blaze of their eyes.

Yeah. That's exactly how I looked at Sissy right now.

I took in my surroundings and planned my attack accordingly. I kicked off my heels and headed in her direction. First, I was going to pull out every single one of her fake hair extensions. Next, the yanking of the spanks. I was going to pull those suckers down to her ankles and push her over before she got her footing. For the finale, I was going to dump the punchbowl all over her, *including the fruit at the bottom.* On second thought, maybe I'd start with the punchbowl.

I glanced at said punchbowl now and back at the Devil's spawn. I narrowed my eyes into two slits, nodded my head at her that it was officially on, and headed for that punchbowl.

To her credit, she was able to translate that.

In fact, she hiked up her dress and scooted her butt out of the ballroom at record speed, screaming all the way.

The last of the lingering crowd broke into a murmur as they craned their necks to watch her go.

Sissy disappeared into the night, and if it had been at all a truly karmic world, she would've had some flying house land on top of her, and I could've taken her ruby slippers and clicked my butt home.

I gathered as much dignity as possible and raised my head high. Devlin was surrounded by three ex-girlfriends, all yelling at him at once.

Carol nodded to me in support, and I felt a little better to see that she appeared to harbor no bad feelings toward me.

I glanced at Mr. Somerset, and his face was neutral. I'm not a psychic, so I had no idea what that meant. But, I did know this was definitely the time to make a hasty retreat.

I did an awkward bow for some unknown reason and ran out of there as quickly as possible.

Like a big old baby. I ran right out of the ball and down the snowy path and away from all those questioning eyes.

I kept running and running, and I didn't care that it was cold and dark. I didn't care about anything but getting as far away from the ball and our horrid lie forever. To my credit, my gown did this floaty lofty thing behind me that I'm sure looked impressive as I ran, at least.

Chapter 43

1 was almost finished packing when Devlin let himself

into our room. "I'm sorry I messed this whole thing up," I said, afraid to meet his eyes.

"I'm so ashamed I lied to all those good people and your father. I need to talk to him. I hope he won't hold my father responsible, whatever we…"

Devlin put a tender finger to my mouth.

I stopped talking, and he looked at me seriously.

He put his hands on my shoulders. "My father already knows the truth. I told him everything before the ball when we were getting our tuxes fit."

"I don't understand. I'm so confused."

He gathered me into his arms. "I took your advice. I told him the truth. No regrets."

My mouth dropped open, but I recovered quickly. I cleared my throat. "You listened to me?"

He nodded.

"I told my father the truth of what I was facing at the company and how hard I'd been working—and that I needed him to trust me whether I was marrying the chauffeur's daughter or not."

I pulled away and looked up at him. "So, your father knows who I am?"

Devlin nodded. "You're not going to believe it, but I think that old coot was playing us."

I smiled.

"But when Sissy brought out Sofia and Vanessa and all the others…"

My eyes widened. "There were more."

Devlin shook his head. "It looked like a Ms. Universe pageant in there."

I put my hands to my head. He gently took them down and into his hands. He smiled lightly at me and said in a reassuring tone, "The point is, my father already knew the truth of why we had faked our engagement, and when Sissy pulled that act at his Mistletoe Ball, my father had had enough."

I closed my eyes and said a quick thank you to God. Somehow, my father wouldn't take any heat for my stupid mistakes.

"Allie, you were right about so many things. I had our accountant run the numbers on that hemp alternative you suggested."

Devlin grabbed me and lifted me up off the ground like a feather. He spun me around gleefully, smiling from ear to ear.

"You're brilliant. Hemp! All the creative geniuses I have working for me, and it took *you* to figure it out."

He dropped me down slowly and looked at me with light bouncing off his eyes. New crinkles appeared around his cheeks I'd never seen before as he brimmed over with the news.

"I'm glad I could be part of it."

A strange silence hung. It seemed our deal had been successful.

I bit my lip.

"Well, if everything is settled, I'm going to get my stuff packed…"

"But…" Devlin began.

I wiped away the tears that sprang to my eyes and pulled myself up tall. "I'd like to go home and spend…what's left of Christmas…with my dad. If that's okay."

Devlin nodded.

I looked down at my hand. "Well, I guess our deal is over. I'm officially single again." I forced a smile.

Devlin's face scrunched up in a thought I couldn't read. "Right. Well…that ring never suited you anyway. I always took you for the sapphire type. No man could want to marry you without celebrating those eyes in jewels."

He gazed into my eyes, and I trembled at the feeling I saw reflected there. But what did it matter? Life had dealt our hands. I was a chauffeur's daughter; he was a billionaire. Our charade was over, and it was time to go home to reality.

He went over to his desk and pulled out a pen and came back with a solemn look. He held out a check. "Here's the check I owed you. You earned it."

I swallow hard as I looked down at the check—two hundred thousand dollars. I had done it. I had saved our house. My father was going to be so happy.

"Thanks," I mumbled. I put the check in my purse and felt my tongue grow big like a stranger in my mouth. I had nothing left to say. The dream was over. The fake love complete. Except for one thing.

I looked up at Devlin.

"If your dad already signed the company over to you before the ball…" I shook my head, trying to understand. I was so confused.

"You didn't have to act like we were in love… why did you dance with me like that and kiss me– like that?"

He looked me in the eye.

"Because I wanted to."

I blushed. Was he messing with me? Trying to get me to break down and throw myself into his arms and kiss those luscious lips again and melt into utopia...

He caught me up in his arms and pulled me close. "Because you're adorable and delightful, and a pain in the butt, and you've changed me."

He pulled me into his arms, and I fell into his spell against my will. I wrapped my arms around him and held on tight and felt every bit of his muscled body pressing against me. His insistent lips kissed me deeply, and I returned his passion.

There was a loud rapping on the door, and we both turned startled by broken silence and our tender moment being burst. I had to catch my knees from buckling.

Sofia's shrill voice cut through the heavy door. "Devlin? We need to talk right now. You get that chauffeurs daughter out of here, and you stop playing games."

Devlin looked at me.

"I better go deal with this and other problems I left at the Ball. "

I nodded. He grabbed my hand again.

"We'll talk later."

And with that, he walked out the door.

Chapter 44

*T*he rooster was crowing when I let myself out of the

bedroom in the early light of Christmas morning. Devlin had come in sometime in the late hours and was fast asleep, luckily. I didn't think I could face him again. I shut the door quietly and snuck one last lingering look at his slumbering figure.

I had changed into my own clothes and tied my hair up in a ponytail. I was sporting my *Hug a Tree* shirt and some jeans, and I almost felt like myself again. I left behind all the clothes Devlin had bought me, as well as the beautiful ball gown with a thank you note for the Landers.

I regretted I wouldn't have time to see Carol and Ethel and wish them a merry Christmas, but I knew it was better this way. I had grown way too attached to the adorable senior bakers for my own good. This was all just acting and the play was over.

Jeeves was kind enough to drive me down the mountain and I blinked away tears randomly swiping at my face with my glove. Jeeves cast sidelong sad glances at me and patted my arm every few minutes. He put on some Christmas music but it sounded odd against the sadness that hung in the air.

He dropped me off at the car rental place, and I hugged him tightly. He patted my back affectionately. "We're all going to miss you, Allie. Please come back."

I wiped back a tear and hugged him one more time before I got out of the car with my backpack. Didn't he realize I was never coming back? The game was over. The deal done. It was time to step out of this bizarre fantasy and go back to my real life.

Jeeves waved goodbye and blew a kiss as he pulled away. I watched him climb the steep incline back up the mountain with a heavy heart. I would miss him.

I looked at the Rolls and hesitated.

I had the key, so there was nothing stopping me now.

I took a deep breath and looked around the town of Kissing Bridge once more, imprinting it upon my memory of things I would love forever, and then I climbed in and drove away.

Chapter 45

1 let myself cry. Why not? I felt as if I had fallen off a

cloud of my own making. I wanted to see the Landers and have them pat me on the back and tell me to take some baked goods and everything would be fine. I wanted my father to hug me and say I had done the right thing. I had saved our home. I wanted Devlin to...

Horns began blaring, and I looked in my back mirror. Devlin was behind me in the black jeep. I bit my lip. He pulled up next to me and motioned me over to the side.

I took a deep breath and pulled over. He jumped out of the jeep and was by my side in a moment. I got out of the limo and closed the door. We were the only ones on the road, and the flurries had picked up again. Little snowflakes danced around Devlin's gorgeous face, and it took everything in me to look away.

"Where are you going?" He took in my clothes and hair.
"Home. I told you. The deal is over. I'm sure Sofia would rather I not be at Christmas with the family, anyway."
He let his breath out hard.
"Balderdash. I could care less about Sofia–or any of those girls." He wrapped his arms around me and pulled me close. "I hate the idea of not spending Christmas with you."
I shook my head. "You do? Why?"
He wrapped his arms around me. "Because you're a breath of fresh air, Allie, and I've gotten used to you insulting me."
I laughed, but it hurt inside. "I need to go home…see my dad." I couldn't meet his eyes.
He tipped my chin up to gaze at me. "If you must go home to see your father, I won't stand in your way, but you have to open up your Christmas gift at least." He reached into his pocket and withdrew an envelope and handed it to me.
I opened the envelope; it was full of legal papers I couldn't make out. I stuffed them back in the container.
"What is this?"
"It's a deed to a penthouse apartment on 5th Avenue."

"Excuse me?"

"A home—for you. You wanted that more than anything."
He smiled from ear to ear.

"I have a home, Devlin. I told you that's what the money
was for."

He grabbed hold of me and pulled me into him and
kissed me deep and hard.

"But not a home in the city—and not near me."

His gray eyes danced.

"I'm confused."

He smiled and grabbed my hands.

"I want to continue to see you, silly."

I stiffened and pulled back. "So, it's another offer?"

He searched my eyes.

"No, Allie. I guess it's the first step. I just want to be
closer to you. That's all I know. We're both horrible at
love. But we're perfect for each other. A mortgage is
almost a commitment." He laughed that deep, sexy
sound, and I would have melted any other time. I was
crazy about him despite all my attempts to deny it, but not
this time.

"I want to keep seeing you, Allie."

I shook my head. "You care about me. I know you do. I'll
surround you with jewels and cars and flowers and let you
protest in front of my building without arresting you…"

I pushed him away from me.

"Are you nuts? Stop fooling yourself. You're Devlin
Somerset, darn bachelor of the year! It's a glorious,

beautiful thing that your father has accepted you for who you are…" I shook my head.

"But I can't lie to myself, Devlin! You are the worst thing that could happen to me. I'm not going to fall in love with you. Let you break my life apart someday when you move on. You're commitment-phobic, and I…I want the real thing." I was surprised at my own truth.

He tried to kiss away my excuses, and I struggled not to give in. I couldn't stop the tears now as my authentic, true self had finally won out.

He wiped them away gently. "I've changed since I met you, Allie."

I gurgled a half-laugh cry out." I don't want you to change, nor do I think you really can, Devlin." I looked at him in those beautiful eyes. "I care about you–I do. But I want the real thing. I was lying to everyone the last four days, but mostly I lied to myself. I don't want to go through life without having real love. I know now more than ever that I want my own family to make Christmas traditions with—and to insult over breakfast."

He laughed stiffly, but I could see sadness creeping into his eyes, and his smile seemed forced.

I took his hands and made him meet my gaze. "I don't want to have any regrets."

I touched his cheek. He looked at me sadly. "Thank you, Devlin. Without you, I might have lied to myself and kept myself from being truly happy."

"Allie…" It came out like a groan. My heart melted.

There were tears in his eyes. "I'll give you the world. Just tell me what can I do?"

He looked so sad; I almost threw myself into his arms and changed my mind. Lied to myself.

He rushed on pleading. "Take the penthouse, it's worth a few million dollars. Cash it in if you want, travel the world, or new clothes."

I shook my head and looked down at myself in my *Hug a Tree* shirt. Devlin would never understand me, nor what truly mattered in my world. The important thing was that now I *did*.

"Donate it to the Amazon, Devlin," I said, and I reached up and kissed him on the cheek.

I got in the limo and sped away as fast as I could before I lost my resolve.

Chapter 46

Three months later

It was spring, and the roses were starting to bloom outside, but the flowers in the yard didn't bring me the joy they had in the past. Random things and memories jumped up and reminded me of Devlin like a ghost. Which, in essence, he was.

Dead to me.

Living in another world.

For the last three months, I had fought a war in my head over my feelings for Devlin. Sometimes it was easier to lie to myself and believe he loved me and that he would suddenly magically change because of our special bond. But I knew life didn't work like that.

Movies and books worked like that.

Real-life gave you lemons, not fairytales.

There was a time when I might have given into Devlin's calls and flowers and cute texts, but not this time. If I let Devlin in, and he acted just as I expected Devlin Somerset would, – it would kill me. Worst of all it would be all my fault.

In the past, I had been side-swiped by the breakup train because I never saw it coming. Now I knew better. I knew certain guys rode that train, but that if I chose a healthy guy, then real love was possible. I wasn't lying to myself anymore. No more fostering commitment-phobic men until they left. I wanted to find my forever love.

Today I was the lead speaker downtown at a rally to support the boycott of palm oil. Palm oil products are just stupid. The toxic oil is poisonous for people and the planet. Sadly, half the loss of the Amazon rainforest is due to palm oil companies buying it up and burning it down to clear it for their palm oil plants. Needless to say, I was passionate about it, and I also truly needed a cause to fill the void that seemed to be where my heart used to live.

I stuffed my backpack with my *Save the Rainforest* bumper stickers and looked around the house. I had everything I needed. I had kept myself as busy as possible, and today was no different. Dad was in the living room, reading the paper when he called to me in an excited voice.

"Allie, you should see this. Somerset Industries has introduced a whole new green agenda for their products." He held up the paper and showed me a picture of Devlin shaking hands with some men in suits.

I caught my breath at seeing his familiar face. Memories of me tangled in his arms, hearts beating together, more alive than ever after our horrific brush with death.

I headed for the door. "See you later, Dad."

Six months later ...

Summer on the Jersey Shore is a wondrous thing. The glorious sun warms the skin and lightens the sorrows. My friends had planned a beach day, and I was tempted to go, but I had a park to protect.

Between finishing grad school and getting our finances back in order, I had kept myself busy enough to avoid my thoughts. But now that I had graduated, I had too much time on my hands. I had begun doubling down on my charity and activist activity while I looked for a job. I didn't need to be lounging around the beach and letting my thoughts wander.

Devlin had finally stopped trying to contact me and I was happy about it.

At least that's the lie I told myself.

I still cried randomly when things reminded me of Devlin, but I was getting over him, really.

I knew I had to cut it off completely. If I let him in a little bit, then I would not be able to remain strong. It hurt badly now, but it would get better someday and I would still have my heart intact.

I took a deep sigh and put my hand to my heart. Who was I kidding?

I came into the kitchen, and Dad was on his iPad. I was dressed in a beautiful blue suit, and Dad whistled.

"I would give you anything you wanted in that outfit." He beamed.

I smiled. "Thanks, Dad. Let's hope the planning committee agrees with you. If all goes well they'll agree that we need more trees planted in that cement block they call a park."

I kissed him on the cheek, and he pointed at the iPad. "Allie, you have to see this. Somerset Industries made a big announcement. They are making all their boxes and envelope products out of hemp."

I raised my eyebrows and leaned over his shoulder. It had pictures of some world business. Devlin was smiling and shaking hands with some other man in a suit outside of Somerset Industries. A beautiful blonde woman was clutching his arm.

I pulled back like I had been stabbed, and Dad looked up at me with a pained expression.

"Sorry, honey, I…"

I patted him on the back. "It's okay, Dad."

I gathered my things and rushed out the door, pushing my feelings down as usual.

Nine months later . . .

 Dad came in from work wearing his chauffeur's uniform and whistled when he saw me. I was dressed up, for me. I wore a form-flattering red dress and some makeup. I had stripped my hair back to its natural color and even bothered to curl it.

 "Honey, you look beautiful." He glowed. "You remind me of your mother."

 "Thanks, Dad." I stopped in the hall mirror and applied some lipstick. "I have another date with Todd. He's a really nice guy." I smiled weakly.

 Dad cleared his throat.

 "I had an interesting passenger today…" He began tentatively.

 I knew where this was going.

 "Dad, I don't want to hear about Devlin– please." I held my hand up.

 "He brought me these." Dad held up some scratch-offs and smiled broadly.

 I shook my head. Scratch-offs, good try Devlin.

 "Maybe you should just take his call, honey?" Dad urged. "He's different since he took over the business. He seems more grown up and ready to settle down."

 Hump! I chortled back a laugh.

"So that's why he had some blonde on his arm in that photo? Devlin Somerset has no heart, he just moves on and grabs another girlfriend just like the playboy he is."

"Nothing like you with Todd."

I looked up quickly. "Exactly."

I slipped on a sweater and grabbed my purse. "I'm looking for the real deal, Dad. I want to be married and have a family and be madly in love - like you and mom."

Dad made a tightly closed smile. "And you deserve that sweetheart. I want the same thing for you. I'm just saying maybe you should give him a chance. People can change, Allie."

I kissed my dad on the cheek and rushed out the door. Dad didn't know Devlin like I did. Devlin Somerset would never change.

Chapter 47

Christmas morning

*D*ad was planted in front of the TV, and I was in charge of Christmas breakfast. It was just the two of us, so we had decided to be complete bums and stay in our pajamas all day.

I was making eggs Benedict with a twist. Instead of the usual hollandaise sauce, I was making the Wellington sauce I had learned from Chef Pierre. It featured tarragon, and it was an unusual combination with the vegetarian version of Benedict I was making—avocado instead of the ham.

Dad was in his Game of Thrones pajamas with his feet up, drinking some hot chocolate in the living room and rubbing off the scratch-offs I had put in his stocking.

"Hey, honey," he called to me." Come see! They're showing pictures of that Mistletoe Ball! Didn't you get to go last year? You should see all the people dressed up. "

I reluctantly went into the living room and glanced at the TV. My heart thumped as I recognized Jeeves and Devlin, of course.

The ball looked as magical as ever.

I returned to my sauce and focused on whisking the eggs so they didn't break. That was the tricky part.

Suddenly, there was a brash pounding at the door.

I backed up, afraid, and peeked through the keyhole, but there was a finger over it. What the heck? We weren't expecting anyone.

I opened the door, and there stood Devlin on a white horse. Next to him were Carol Landers and her husband, Dr. Archibald, Mr. Somerset, Pierre, and Jeeves, too!

I brought my hand to my heart, and instinctively felt for my hair. It was in a tangled bun, and I was still in my Grinch pajamas. Figures.

"What's going on!" I coughed out in surprise as I looked at the group assembled on my porch.

Dad called from the living room. "Allie, you better get in here quick!" I looked at the crew at my door and the horse, then back at my dad.

"Ah, Dad, we've got some visitors…" I looked over my shoulder. "And some guy at the door on a horse!" I said with a frown in Devlin's direction. How dare he fairytale me on Christmas morning? What a low blow.

Dad was yelling for me like he won the lottery as he came in. "You have to see this right away…" He stopped in his tracks when he saw the crew at the door.

"Merry Christmas, Charles," Mr. Somerset said happily.

"Merry Christmas, Harold." Dad's eyebrows rose as he took in the strange group at the door.

"Dad, this is Carol Landers and her husband, the doctor. And this is Pierre the Chef and Jeeves, of course…" He smiled at me.

Dad waved them inside, to my horror.

"Well, come in! Come in. Merry Christmas to you all." He ushered them forward with a giant grin. "You'll want to see this, I'm sure."

Mr. Somerset approached me, and I smiled. He reached out his arms and hugged me. I held on tight and was relieved that he seemed to have forgiven me. He pulled back and looked at me.

"Now this is the beautiful natural girl I remember from the carriage house days." He touched my hair.

"Much better."

I smiled and blushed at the state of my hair piled on my head in a messy bun.

"Oh, and darling, by the way, I took care of Sissy, so I think you're even."

I raised my brows, and he smiled mischievously.

"I informed her that she was getting cut off from her inheritance if she didn't learn to deserve it."

I let my breath out in a gust and rolled my eyes. "Why can't I see Sissy learning to be a better person lounging in her Malibu mansion?"

He patted me on the back. "Oh, no dear. She's in the fields with the farmworkers overseeing the California transition to hemp."

He motioned Jeeves over. Jeeves beamed at me and showed me his phone. On it was a picture of Sissy in dirty overalls, sweating and looking miserable in the hot fields. I looked at them both, and we all started laughing.

This was turning into a great Christmas after all.

Dad played host, and everyone got comfortable in the living room, while I dealt with Devlin. He was standing at the door, waiting on his horse. I looked up at him.

"What are you doing?" I said.

"What I should have done a year ago."

I shook my head and looked over my shoulder. "Please, I don't want to talk about this again."

"I've been thinking–all year, actually."

My eyes met his, and I felt myself starting to spiral into his siren's web. I looked away.

"How exactly does one go about repaying the woman that helped mend the bridge between an estranged son and father? And for saving people's jobs, the environment, and helping our business not only recover, but go on to have record sales?"

I hunched my shoulders. "I'm happy I could help. You didn't have to come all the way over here ...on a horse."

"You're right." He slid off in one athletic move. "And we trailered the horse, actually." Devlin smiled. He tied the reins.

"I came here to give you a Christmas gift."

"A Christmas gift," I repeated numbly. Boy, I was really killing it with the witty conversation. "I told you I don't want anything. Nothing has changed. "

He put up a finger to my lips tenderly. "Actually, I believe there was *one thing* you told me that you did want."

"That you are still incapable of giving me." I threw my hands up in the air. "Don't lie to yourself or me."

Now my father was frantically calling us into the living room. I gritted my teeth. We joined the group gathered on the sectional couch, staring at the TV. Not much I could say now that half of Kissing Bridge was in my living room.

"I don't know what you're trying to pull bringing everyone here," I whispered as we joined them and sat down on the couch next to Carol. She patted my hand, and I smiled at her weakly.

My dad was excited. "Everyone quiet! They're coming back from the commercial."

I chanced a glance at Devlin. He was sitting way too close to me. I could smell his pine cologne and just being near him made me feel weak all over.

"Okay, okay, here we go!" Dad whistled.

The TV switched back to the news, and two reporters were dressed as Santa and Mrs. Clause.

"Now to our big story. We have to report one of the most amazing Christmas gifts maybe ever given."

"Wouldn't you say that, Russell?"

The man on TV nodded. "I would, Joanne. I have to say that I don't think any gift is comparable, and what we are talking about, folks, is this…"

The cameras switched out of the studio to an on-location reporter.

The caption said *Live From The Amazon Rainforest.*

My eyes widened, and Carol reached over beside me and squeezed my hand. The TV showed a drone flying over the glorious trees of the rainforest while the reporters highlighted its diversity and the number of tribes still living there.

Finally, somebody else cares, I thought. I leaned in, excited. Now the on-location reporter dressed as an elf was back with a crowd of local Brazilian people waving and holding signs that read:

"THANK YOU, ALLIE ARCHER!"

I caught my breath and looked around at everyone in the living room. They were all smiling at me.

I stared at the TV, stunned. "Why – why – are they thanking me?"

I choked back my emotions.

The reporter continued. "The largest private acquisition of the Amazon rainforest ever has been bought as a private park to protect it forever for the people of Brazil and the world. Welcome to the first and only of its kind. *Allie Archer Park.*"

The people waved and blew kisses and shouted, "Merry Christmas!"

The reporters signed off with, "Merry Christmas, Allie Archer, and to everyone around the world!"

I brought my hands to my face, and tears burst from my eyes like a fire hydrant that had been run over. What was happening? Was this real or some kind of joke?

I sobbed uncontrollable tears that racked my body and made me hyperventilate. Carol nudged Devlin, and he cleared his throat.

He dropped to his knees in front of me, and put his hands on my face and made me look at him. I sniffled back my ugly cry and fell into his loving gaze.

"I love you, Allie. I didn't think I'd ever say that and mean it to anyone. But I know now I don't want to live without you."

He opened up a box, and there was an engagement ring inside.

I gasped, and through my blurry tears, I could see it was a massive diamond ring with two blue sapphires on each side.

It was stunning and bigger than Sofia's.

I looked around the room and saw the kind faces smiling at us. Mr. Somerset nodded and tilted his head at his son.

I looked back into Devlin's eyes, and him down at my feet. How many times I had wished for this moment? Of course, in the past, I wanted to kill his ego and break his arrogance. Now I just wanted to kiss him.

I threw my arms around him. "Yes. Yes. I'll marry you."

He beamed and slipped the ring on my finger, and we looked down at it together. No fake ring. No fat knuckle. Just us and everyone we loved on Christmas morning to witness the beginning of our real union.

"No regrets." He smiled.

"No regrets," I said.

He whisked me up in the air like a feather and held me there for a moment before dropping me into his arms and kissing me until I couldn't breathe.

"She said, *yes!*" he shouted, raising his arms over his head.

The crowd in the living room stood and applauded wildly. Carol wiped her eyes and Jeeves and Pierre patted each other on the back.

I looked at my dear father and all these people I loved that were my new family. Right then and there I suddenly understood every single mushy Christmas movie I had ever seen.

All the syrupy stuff and impossible things suddenly coming together on Christmas had been another fairytale, like true love, that I wouldn't let myself believe.

But now I know miracles really can happen at Christmas.

Against all odds, a miracle happened to me. Maybe, this Christmas, one could happen for you too.

Merry Christmas, everyone!

Dear friends, I hope you enjoyed my book! Many of the characters featured in this book began their stories in the *Love on Kissing Bridge Series.*

I would be so happy to give you my best selling first book in my sweet and funny holiday romance series for FREE as a gift. It is called, Christmas Kisses and Cookies, and it is the first introduction to the Landers ladies and Kissing Bridge.

FREE JUST WRITE ME:)) Morningmayan@gmail.com

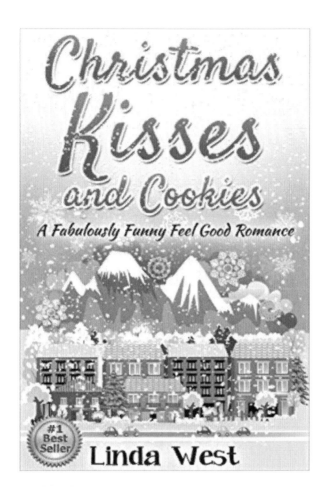

FREE!

Looking for more Kissing Bridge magic? Check out this best selling holiday novel about three women who get a chance to re-do one Christmas in their life...

The Magical Christmas Do Over

A Small Town Second Chance Christmas Romance

LINDA WEST

The
Magical Christmas

Do   Over

By

Linda West

"Once in a blue moon you get a chance to change your life, and this was that blue moon."

CHAPTER 1

It was a cold December eve, some say the coldest in decades, and a blizzard warning was in effect. Being the Friday before Christmas, most of the workers at Kennedy and Crane had already left for the Christmas holiday.

Samantha looked at the clock and groaned inwardly. It was after eight o'clock, and she wanted to go home like everyone else, but her boss, Macy Kennedy was in an extra foul mood even for her.

"Shouldn't you be getting home to put on that awesome Chanel dress you bought for the big night Macy?" Samantha chirped brightly trying to lighten her up.

Macy spun around and glared at her with daggers in her eyes.

"No, I shouldn't be getting home to try on my Chanel dress." She mocked Samantha's syrupy tone.

Her dark brows were knit together and her brown eyes looked black with the size of her pupils. She ran her hands through her short, dark hair and then stared back at Samantha with disbelief.

"I got a text from Todd an hour ago. He's gone off to LA with some friends *for Christmas!*"

Samantha's mouth opened.

"What? Why? Didn't he –" She stopped herself. "I'm sure he has a good reason, Macy."

Macy snorted.

"Yeah, good reasons usually don't come in a text. I'm losing him, Sam."

Macy plopped down in her chair and stared out the large picture window at the oncoming storm. She tapped her long, manicured nails on her desk like a woodpecker. "Says he'll call me when he gets back…in a month."

Samantha's mouth fell open. Poor Macy. It looked like she was getting the ultimate big let down, broken up with at Christmas. No engagement celebration after all.

"Here's a piece of mail you didn't get." Sam said quickly, as she placed it on Macy's sleek metal desk. Mail usually distracted Macy.

"Send it back." Macy said dully without turning.

Samantha continued hopefully. "It's not the annual Christmas invite from your mother Macy, that one is always in a red envelope. I *always* send that back. This is something different."

Samantha looked at the pretty Tiffany blue colored envelope. "It's addressed to you personally, not the company."

Macy cocked her head to one side intrigued.

Sam rushed on eager to bring some sort of happiness to her boss. "Maybe it's a love letter from Todd with two tickets to Paris for when he gets back?"

Macy let out a big huff and gazed out the window at the sheets of snow beginning to fall.

They both knew that wasn't the case. Todd's last minute text was just a breakup in disguise.

But if not Todd, then who? Macy really didn't have any close friends that would send her a Christmas card. Anyone that did know her knew she abhorred Christmas. Too much money being spent in the name of sentimentality and tricky marketers as her father always said.

Macy waved her hand without looking back at Samantha as if she were a servant.

"Read it."

Samantha scanned the letter, then suddenly, caught her breath and brought her hand to her heart.

"Macy."

Something in Samantha's tone made Macy spin her chair around.

"What?"

"It's from a friend of your mothers, a Ms. Carol Landers."

"What? You have got to be kidding me?" Macy threw her hands up in the air. "Now my mother is having her friends write me to beg me to come visit her? How utterly selfish!"

She shook her head. "What is it with her? She ruins my life and then she stalks me. Can't she see no matter how many times she begs me to come home for Christmas, *I'm not going to Kissing Bridge!*"

Samantha swallowed uncomfortably and croaked out, "I'm so sorry, Macy. But this letter says that your mother passed away yesterday, and you're the only relative left to claim her body."

She looked up sadly and met Macy's stunned eyes.

"You have to go home to Kissing Bridge."

Chapter 2

Macy felt an odd sense of nothingness. Instead of sorrow there was a vague grayness that didn't nearly match the depth of feeling called for. Maybe it was regret. Her mother, dead. She hadn't even known she was sick. Then again, she hadn't seen or spoken to her since she was a child. Her mother's big, kind brown eyes flashed across her memory, and she swallowed hard.

She picked up the letter Samantha had put down in front of her and read it.

"Dear Macy, I'm so sorry to tell you that your mother has passed away. Nobody seems to have any contact number for you, and I pray that this letter finds its way to you by the grace of God. Please come home to Kissing Bridge to

collect her remains because we don't know what to do with her body.
Sincerely and with great sorrow,
Carol Landers."

Macy didn't move for a moment, and it seemed as if time stopped.

Even in death her mother was managing to ruin her life. She closed her eyes to shut out the truth, and squash down all of her feelings, like a fly that needed to be swatted.

Feelings were weakness her father had always taught her. Feelings hindered your life, not helped. Stick to the bottom line, work hard and it would pay off. That was his motto. Where it had become hers she didn't know. She felt a panic attack coming on again.

Just then, the maid opened the door and walked into Macy's office, not realizing people were still in the building. Happy holiday music followed in her wake through the crack in the door and her jaunty red bell earrings jingled as she walked.

"Oh!" She stopped dead at seeing the big boss and her personal assistant still at the office. "Sorry! I thought y'all were gone like everyone else in the building."

Macy spun her chair around, her brown eyes flashing in anger. She glowered at the poor woman and looked her up and down, trying to find the source of the tinkling, festive sound.

Macy pinched her dark brows together and rose from her chair, pointing at the offenders hanging from the maid's ears.

"There!"

She turned her anger on Samantha. "Don't we have a company employee dress code?"

Samantha looked the maid's outfit over. She was in the company mandated black uniform with her name, NAOMI, scrawled under the Kennedy and Crane logo.

Samantha straightened. "Of course, Macy. She's wearing black that's the holiday dress code. I sent out memos to the entire staff. I don't see the problem."

Macy pointed at Naomi. "Those – those holiday earrings look ridiculous. It's an embarrassment to the company."

Samantha's eyes widened. "I'll make sure I add it to the original memo and send it off after Christmas, Macy."

The maid looked at Samantha with fear in her large, almond-brown eyes, and she fidgeted, not sure what to do next.

Samantha waved her in further. "It's fine, Naomi. Please come in. Do what you need to do. We don't want to stop you from getting your work done just because we're working overtime."

Macy started pacing across the room like a panther. She was dressed in all black and thin as a rail and looked like she was ready to explode.

She turned her attention to Naomi, who was busy dusting and trying to finish up as quickly as possible so she could make her way safely out of the office and Macy's weird Christmas ire.

"Naomi."

Macy read the nametag and addressed the maid as if seeing her for the first time.

Naomi King stopped and lifted her beautiful eyes to look Macy in the face. She had been working for the office-cleaning agency for five years now, and she'd run into the strict and serious Macy before, but never had been regarded, let alone talked to, by her.

"What are you doing for Christmas? Kids, gifts, all that I guess?" Macy prodded. "Figgy pudding maybe?"

Naomi cocked her head to the side. She didn't need the big boss lady asking questions or giving her the super-stare down right now.

"Got one kid. He's in jail, so I guess I'll go by for a visit. Bring him some cigarettes."

Macy stopped pacing and looked at her.

She was sorry she asked.

A new weather alert suddenly erupted from Samantha's Apple watch and startled her. She pushed at the side controls trying to shut off the irritating warning buzzer reminding them the blizzard was almost upon them.

"So Macy, shall I try and book a flight for you?" Samantha asked. She was bewildered by Macy's lack of reaction to the death of her mother.

"Kissing Bridge, Vermont right?"

Macy nodded. "If I have no other choice."

Naomi spoke up. "There's no way you're getting an airplane out of here. It's been all over the news that all the flights have been canceled for the next three days due to this darn blizzard-of-a-century coming in."

Samantha parried. "Okay, a rental car then."

Macy shook her head. "Like no one else had thought of that alternative on the Friday before Christmas."

Samantha countered. "Right, of course. A car then. I'd lend you mine if I had one, Macy, but who has a car in Manhattan?"

Naomi piped in. "I do."

They both looked at her.

"How much?" Macy said dully.

Naomi cleared her throat. "Well, it's actually my boyfriend's pickup truck, so I'll have to call him."

Samantha shut off her watch and sighed. She had already gotten three warnings on her phone about the oncoming blizzard. She was eager to get home like everyone else, but it rarely mattered what Samantha wanted.

Samantha Henderson just did what others requested.

She had survived her entire life that way, and the last ten years of being the Boss-from-Hades' right hand lady.

Everyone else who had ever had the misfortune of working for Macy Kennedy was fired within months, sometimes weeks. One poor girl never made it through the first day. But if nothing else, Samantha was a survivor.

The law office had moved uptown, Macy had been made partner, and Samantha followed and kept her head down. Partially to avoid the caustic moods of her temperamental boss, but also to shield her facial deformity from curious eyes.

Samantha was a natural beauty, with large green eyes tinged with dark lashes and cheekbones to die for. Her hair was a soft blonde and it hung nearly to her waist, with long side bangs styled perfectly to mask the left side of her face as much as possible.

Still, if one looked a bit closer, they would see that the side of Samantha's pretty face was smashed inward all along the left side of her face, with a maroon lighting thin scar that ran the length of it.

It didn't make Samantha ugly, but it made her strange.

Unnatural.

Different.

It wasn't people's faults they stared. Sam had come to understand that people did that when they encountered something they weren't accustomed to. She had gotten used to the staring over the years, but the damage to her face was not the worst of her disabilities.

Chapter 3

Naomi rang her boyfriend and clenched her hands. It'd been a few hours since her last session, and she hadn't expected the bosses to still be hanging around the office at this late hour. She usually had the place to herself, and she could pop her pills while no one was looking.

Once she was high, Naomi felt normal and able to go about her mundane, thoughtless routine of cleaning the affluent offices of Kennedy and Crane until the wee hours of the morning. After that she would go home to her big dose and the awaiting peace of slumber before it started again.

Where was that loser Kiki? Totally like him to *not* be around when they had a sweet deal like this just fall into their laps. If she worked this right she could get a ripe good deal out of Ms. High-and-Mighty Kennedy.

Kiki picked up.

His voice was hoarse and he sounded out of it.

"*Kiki,*" Naomi whispered urgently despite the fact that she was alone. She looked over her shoulder. "I got us an epic setup to make some easy cash off my psycho boss woman. Her momma done croaked and she needs a ride home."

Kiki seemed to brighten. "And? What's it got to do with me?"

Naomi released her breath. "I need your truck for a couple days, until Monday at the most."

"No way."

Naomi knew only cash and his next pill purchase, which often went together, motivated her boyfriend.

"She'll pay five hundred bucks," Naomi lied.

She planned to ask Macy for a lot more than that, but she wasn't about to let that on to Kiki. She knew Macy was over the barrel with no options and she planned to milk the situation for all it was worth.

Naomi had a kid in jail that the lawyer said he could help if she only had the money. She was going to ask Macy for two thousand dollars, help her son, and maybe get a little place for herself that didn't include Kiki.

CHAPTER 4

Naomi returned to the office. "He said he'd be happy to help."

Samantha brightened, but Macy glowered at her. Clearly the thought of six hours of driving to pick up her disowned mother's body was going to be too much for her to handle.

… "but he wants two thousand," Naomi finished.

Macy let out a big laugh. "Of course he does. Not like I have any options! Right, Naomi?"

Naomi cast her big almond eyes down.

"Not really, ma'am."

"Have you heard of price gouging?"

Naomi looked at Samantha, then back at Macy. She shook her head. "No, ma'am."

Macy threw her hands up. "Well, it appears I have no choice, so go get this golden vehicle I'm renting us for the exorbitant price of $2,000 and let's go!"

Samantha looked up. "Excuse me? Us?"

Macy waved her off with one hand. "Go home and pack. Naomi, you too. Then come get us in this rented chariot and let's get on with this miserable nonsense."

Samantha caught her breath. "But – but it's Christmas weekend, Macy! We spend it with Harold's parents every year. I can't –"

Macy patted her on the back. "Afford to lose your job? We both know sweet Harold doesn't make enough as a dental salesman for all those tests you need."

Samantha's eyes flashed with anger and she bit her tongue so hard she tasted blood, but she kept her face calm. How dare Macy use that against her? She'd only told Macy the truth of her condition because she'd burst into tears last week over the failed results again, and the impending future of not having enough money to retry in vitro fertilization.

Samantha decided she was *just going to say no.*

"I'm so sorry, Macy, but I just can't go. Christmas is really important to Harold."

Macy glanced up.

"I'll pay you twenty thousand dollars to go with me, Samantha."

She rose from her seat, walked over, and took both of Samantha's hands.

"Handle this for me…. Please Sammy. I can't do this without you. And you need the money; you know you do. Maybe this time it will take?" Macy's eyes softened as she

298   My Billionaire Fake Fiancé

stared into Samantha's green orbs. "I know how much it means to you both. Harold will understand."

Samantha shook her head. This was so typical. Over the years, Samantha had put up with untold difficulties being Macy's right hand girl. Harold thought she was horrible, and begged Sam to quit years ago. But Samantha had outlasted eight of Macy's boyfriends, three best friends, and twenty assistants. By default, Samantha was possibly the longest relationship Macy had ever had.

Sam took a deep breath. She knew Macy meant well, and that she hid her vulnerability underneath all her bark and bite. Even though she came across as harsh and cold, Macy had a good side down deep, very deep, inside.

Samantha softened. Poor Macy had just lost her mother.

"I'll have to talk to Harold."

Macy nodded. Naomi opened her mouth to complain, but Macy put a hand up to stop her.

"And before you go saying no and leaving us alone with your boyfriend's jalopy – I'll pay you an additional $3,000 to drive us up there and back."

Naomi's eyes went large. "You got yourself a driver."

This is the end of this excerpt!

Buy now!

Click here!

The complete set of Love on Kissing Bridge Mountain series is available NOW on Amazon.

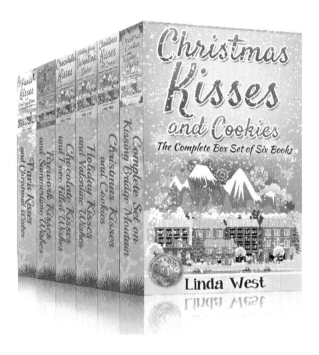

Thank you so very much for reading my books!
P.S.
If you *didn't like* my book PLEASE write me directly with your thoughts and ideas on how I can make my books more enjoyable for you! I work very hard as a self-published author to bring quality and low-priced books out for my readers. I truly value all feedback good and bad! Thank you!
Write me directly at
Morningmayan@gmail.com
If you loved my book – PLEASE leave a few words in a review on Amazon)
Thank you so very much! Wishing you happiness and sunshine!
Love,
Linda

If you haven't read the first book in the Kissing Bridge Cozy Mystery series please check it out!

The fun starts when Kat moves back home and begins working for the magical Landers sisters.

Trouble boils over when a crockpot goes missing at the big Chili- Cook off and a body is found.

https://www.amazon.com/dp/B071VBV9PJ

What people are saying about:

DEATH
by
Crockpot

"Side-split tingly funny and great little thriller. West gives Evanovich a run for her money. Loved this book. Can't wait for the next. Thank you!"

Posie Arnold Entertainment Now

"A gripping fun suspense thriller and cozy mystery. Set in a small ski town and centered around a magical bakery. This is humorous American literature at its best."

Dan Collins Dartmouth

"5***** "Funny! I laughed out loud. This book is unique and page turning. Highly recommended!"

S. Sprawling FutureTrends

"A humorous lighthearted cozy mystery that is full of suspense and twists and turns that will leave you laughing and surprised. Kat O'Hara returns home penniless, heartbroken and without a job. When the magical Landers sisters hire her to run their new Enchanted Cafe little do they suspect that a gruesome murder is about to take place in their small town of Kissing Bridge Mountain. Things bubble over at the big chili cook-off when a crockpot goes missing and a body is found. Loved it!"

Joy Stella Buffalo, NY

"5****** Love these characters and so happy to see them return in another fun series! What a treat. Keep writing about Kissing Bridge please!"

Dawn Deviso, Youngstown

Secrets the Secret Never Told You

The Balanced Body Diet

5 Steps to Manifest

The Triangle Plan

To Heaven and Back

I would be so happy to give you the my best selling first book in my sweet and funny holiday romance series for FREE as a gift. It is called, Christmas Kisses and Cookies, and it is the first introduction to the Landers ladies and Kissing Bridge.

FREE JUST WRITE ME:)) Morningmayan@gmail.com

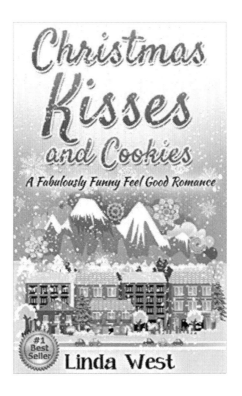